SPECIAL

KENDRA ROBINSON
RONETTE CLARKE WILLIAMS
MARKEISHA SHORTER

FOR ALL THE LOVE AND SUPPORT AS I WORKED THROUGH MY CRAZY TO FINALLY WRITE THIS STORY.

IMMORTAL BLACK: RISING
BY M.X.ROBIN

Throughout history, the black race has been enslaved, marginalized, and mistreated. Their culture, art, inventions, and beliefs were destroyed or claimed by other races as their own. They were taken from their birth lands and scattered all over the world either by force or trickery but only rarely ever by choice. The word slavery appears in their collective history more than it does in that of any other race.

In modern times they are led to believe that they have better lives than at any time before it. Not realizing that they are still slaves. Not remembering the freedoms, they once had. Not understanding that the laws that claim to give everyone justice are just invisible chains around their neck. Not understanding that those who enforce it are the ones holding the whip if they get out of line and ax if they forget their place. They see how some seem to rise above their station to eat at the table instead of out of the dirt, not realizing that most of these people are just puppets used to give others hope. Their talents are used to entertain instead of uplift or defend.

When they are slaughtered like animals, they are left to bury their dead and shed their tears. They scream that black lives matter, but the world doesn't listen. They march in the streets screaming that if there is no justice there will be no peace, but the powers that be just send their enforcers to put them back in place. Finally, they resort to violence using the weapons and tactics of their oppressors. The world takes notice and calls them animals and savages. They use it as a reason to butcher them and they mask it, as necessary. People of the same race take to the Internet and the television in order to not only separate themselves from but also to demonize those of their own race who have simply said they have had enough. But, in the end, no matter how much they struggle none of them have the will to break the chains. No one has the will to stand up fully and take up the mantle of a leader who doesn't simply ask for their people's freedom but is willing to take it by force. There have been many who thought they had the will, but they were crushed because they could not take the step over that final line and break that last chain.

I have spent an age watching my race crumble from the status of King and Queens to little more than animals in the eyes of the world. Watching as the land of our birth was slowly turned into a cesspit used as the world's garbage dump. I have watched as my people were preyed on by not only other races but their own race. I have watched from the shadows building my power and influence until it was time to strike. Never showing my true self to any but those who shared my vision. Even though the struggle of my people brought tears to my eyes, I waited, watched, and built. Now, in the year 2050, the wait is over. I was given the gift of immortality by a force I myself cannot begin to understand and one single purpose: Change the world so that not only the black race can taste true freedom and equality but all races. I have gone by many names through many thousands of years. I have experienced love and lose more times than any other man alive or dead. I have never been given the gift of a child, that was one of the many sacrifices I had to make to serve my purpose.

Now, I am called Bryson Kane and I am the richest man alive. I own multiple companies the largest being the tech giant Black Tide. I have connections in every country on Earth and with these, I have built an organization more powerful than any nation. Now, it is time to unleash the Tide on the most powerful and most corrupt nation on Earth: America.

PART ONE

CHAPTER 1

United States President Gerald Deckland sits in the Oval Office watching the United News Network reporting on the riots going on around the country in the wake of the Portland Massacre. As usual U.N.N pulled no punches putting the blame squarely on the shoulders of the Federal Police and of course Gerald's administration. No one seemed to lay any blame on the terrorist of the Black Lives Matter movement who had opened fire on the officers who had just been there to protect the Portland Federal Police Headquarters. After seeing no less than five of their own go down the officers retaliated in self-defense. They did not know who the shooters were, so they opened fire on the entire crowd. By the end of it one-hundred and sixteen people were dead in total and of course every minute of it was caught on camera. Now, a month later it was played on every news network worldwide, every social media site and video streaming service. The country was literally in flames as people took to the streets in every major city in protest. Then the protest turned to riots and looting. It was a repeat of the nightmare year 2020. Gerald turns off the TV as they start talking about how black people are being systematically targeted by the Federal Police.

He closes his eye and massages his temples. When he opened his eyes, he saw that the eyes of everyone there were on him. This cabinet meeting had been going on for nearly four hours now. They had been there to discuss what steps they needed to take to save their country. Gerald had planned to go golfing after this but had decided he would rather spend the rest of the day in the White House spa as his skin had become far too pale for his liking. He runs his figures through his thick blonde hair and sits back in his chair.

"I am declaring martial law." Gerald says looking around the room to see everyone reactions. "This has gone on long enough and now it is time to enact Sanction 45. This is not the first time our country has been under threat by those hiding behind the flag of fighting social injustice. We will not be bullied, and we will not stand by while our laws are broken. If they want to turn against the country that has fed and protected them that is fine. We will treat them like the animals they are."

He stands and walks to the middle of the room. Looks around at all the white faces staring at him some of them in the room and others on screens set into the walls of the office. Some were political figures and others were CEOs of the country's largest businesses. All of them were true patriots and the backbone of his great country. They had all worked hard to get where they were and didn't waste their time moaning about how unfair the world was. They didn't sit and wait for the government to fed them or beg for more money they never had to work for. These were true Americans.

"Taking these steps will make them demonize us, but I think we are all use to that right now." Gerald is still looking at their faces to see how they were receiving his message. "In the end our nation will be saved and stronger than ever before. We will put the worst of the animals in cages and let them be examples of what will happen to the rest. I know that no one ever expected to have to go this far. But my predecessor saw that these laws may have been needed. He saw this day coming and now it is time to use what he gave us."

The room was silent for a while and then his Secretary of Defense Henry Blake stood and started clapping. This was followed by his Vice President Fred March and then he was surrounded by applause. He smiled and shook hands around the room. When this was over, he would sign an order that would destroy over a hundred years of civil progress and return the United States back to the time of slavery.

In the corner of the room stood another individual. This one was white as well, but it had no gender and no emotions. It is a BT-98 the latest model of humanoid robots created by Black Tide Industries. This particular model is a combat model made specifically for the United States Secret Service. They had ordered nearly five hundred just like it. All of whom had been studied, programmed and approved for use by the smartest minds at DARPA.

But, even the most secure groups were not safe from the influence of the Tide, and through the eyes of the BT-98, the entire meeting was watched and recorded.

Atlanta Federal Police Officer Colleen Johnson stares at the angry mob standing across from her and her fellow officers who stood behind the barricade built across Peachtree Street. The officers are in full riot gear and stand behind walls of both stationary and portable energized riot shields. They are backed up by water cannon trucks as well as BT-98 Lawbots.

The riots had been going on for over a month now in response to the Portland Massacre. So far, this group of about three hundred had done no damage but they all knew how fast that could change. Things could go from yelling and sign waving to downtown Atlanta going up in flames. It had already happened in other major cities like Houston and Miami. Protest were how they all started.

Atlanta is one of the most popular cities in America and since the early 2000s, it had been one of the fastest growing. It was home to well over ten million people now well over half of that number are African American. Over the last twenty years, the number of African American deaths not only in Atlanta but all across the state of Georgia has tripled. The way the news reported it these numbers are caused by gang and domestic violence. But in reality, more blacks have been killed by law enforcement over that time period than any other method of violence.

This was a statistic Colleen knew well because she had done her part to add to it. In the four years since she graduated from the academy, she has killed ten people eight of them were black and two Mexican. All of them had been gangbangers and drug dealers. But that had mattered little to the public, all they saw was the fact that she had killed people of color. It didn't even matter that she was black herself, they still demonized and shunned her. Her own family wanted nothing to do with her and that was something she learned to live with.

She had sworn an oath to protect and serve the citizens of the United States when she accepted her badge. How was it hers or any of her fellow officer's fault that more people of color decide to be criminals or don't comply?

Since its founding in the year 2021, the United States Federal Police Force has handled all domestic law enforcement. The FBI, DEA, ATF, and most of the other domestic agencies along with every police department in the country had been combined to form it. Since that time crime has been cut in half. There were no more inner departmental bickering and they got things done. The drug flow from Mexico which had once been a flood was now a trickle, they had clamped down on gang violence and even white-collar crime. So, they had done what they were made to do. In the process, they had to break quite a few eggs colored and white. Yes, it was true that they were able to actually arrest more white criminals than any other race but, that was just how things played out. Some people wanted to take their chances in court while others wanted to be Billy Badass.

So, as she looked at the cheering chanting mob of protestors most of whom were the same color as her, Colleen didn't feel any pity.

"Black lives matter!"

"No justice no peace!"

"We shouldn't die because of the color of our skin!"

These were all lines she had heard since childhood. She thought the same thing now as she did then: empty words. She had grown up in a poor neighborhood and watched people of her so-called proud race spend days killing each other, getting high, or being lazy bums waiting for the next government handout. Even her own family disgusted her. Her mother spent all day working a dead-end job and her father who was a disabled army veteran spent his days whining about how life wasn't fair in between bottles. She had worked hard to get out of there. When she finally graduated high school and went to college, she got to see how people with the same mindset as she lived. They worked hard and devoted their lives to be productive citizens of their country. It didn't matter what color they were; they didn't let it stop them or whine about not having it handed to them. When she looked at the mob of protesters coming towards her all she saw were terrorists and all she heard was anti-American bullshit. All lives mattered except for the ones who did not obey the law.

"This is your final warning!" her commanding officer yells through the speakers of the trucks. "This area is off-limits, if you come any closer, we will be forced to open fire and make arrests."

The mob did not slow as they marched towards the wall of officers. Colleen's grip tighter on her gun. It was loaded with stun rounds like everyone else. When fired they hit their targets and hit them with a shock strong enough to temporarily disrupt their nervous systems. If they hit a target in the face or too may rounds hit the same target, they could cause permanent damage or even death. But again, all these people had to do was obey the law and go home. Instead, they kept coming. Colleen would be going home to her husband and children, that was a promise. If she had to be the cause that one of these terrorist did not, she was fine with that.

"No justice no peace!" Victoria Vaga yells as she marches at the front of the protest.

She is a part of the Atlanta chapter of Black Lives Matter. They have marched over ten miles so far today with more and more people joining their ranks every mile. But still this march was much smaller than they had hoped for. Victoria knew it was because many of their members had gotten tired of the Atlanta B.L.M's methods. They still believed violence only begets violence and refused to do anything but march and protest.

The Portland Massacre had been the spark needed to light the fire and now many of their people were turning to the ranks of black militant groups like Black First and Won't Turn. Victoria is half black and half Latino, she had spent the majority of her life in the church. Her father is a Baptist pastor, and her mother is a lifelong catholic. She had the Bible drilled into her in three separate languages English, Spanish, and Latin. But she understood anger. Her stepbrother Greg had been in Portland and he was now paralyzed from the waist down thanks to a bullet to his spine. She had spent the last month helping her parents move him back to their home in Lithia Springs, Georgia. This was her first march since it all happened. So, she knew what it was like to be angry, but she still believes in God. Whenever anger threatens to overwhelm her, she quotes Romans 12:19 to herself.

"Beloved, never avenge yourselves, but leave it to the wrath of God, for it is written, vengeance is mine, I will repay, says the Lord."

So, she fought violence with peace and lies with truth. They had planned to march all the way to the steps of city hall but at about mile seven Victoria had noticed the lack of traffic. She had been in enough marches to know that meant the police were redirecting traffic. Now her fears were confirmed as she saw the line of federal police in front of them. A male voice warned them to turn around or face the consequences. They kept marching forward and she pulled out her phone and sends a message to the group chat.

"We need to divert our route."

Others were saying the same thing and then all the messages simply disappeared. Victoria looked at her phone in confusion. Then a message appeared. The name attached to it is Wolves.

"Do not fear and do not turn. We are with you now no one will harm you."

Victoria read the message again and again. Then she felt someone push past her. She looked up and saw a tall man in a black hoodie, cargo pants, and boots step in front of her. He was not alone more men and women in black stepped forward until they led the march. They all raised their fist in the air and started a new chant.

"Tide! Tide! Tide! We rise!"

The chant rose behind her as well until it drowned out all the others. Then it replaced them as others in the group took it up. Victoria didn't even realize she was yelling it as well.

"Tide! Tide! Tide! We rise!"

Colleen watched as the figures in black hoodies stepped in front of the mob. They have their hoods up and their faces are covered by what looked like hockey masks. They raise their gloved fists in the air and started a new chant.

"Tide! Tide! Tide! We rise!"

Soon the entire mob was cheering it. It was not like the other cheers this was almost a war chant. Then the speakers on the water truck started broadcasting it behind the police line. It wasn't the voice of the commander; this voice was much deeper. It was being played over the helmet comms and they couldn't hear anything else. Colleen attempted to talk and then tried to turn off the comm, but nothing worked. Finally, she reached up and removed her helmet, her senses were now assaulted by the chanting of the approaching mob and the trucks' speakers.

"What the hell was this?" Colleen thought. "Had they been hacked? No, that was impossible their systems ran the latest DARPA software, and that shit was unbreakable."

She turned and looked at her patrol partner Luke Harp. He is a big white guy with a blonde mohawk that was currently lying flat from his helmet. He had yanked his helmet off a few seconds after her.

"What the hell is this?" he asked out loud echoing her thoughts.

"Your guess is as good as mine."

She raised her gun again and took aim. To her surprise, the crowd had stopped now. The front row of figures in hoodies no longer had their fist in the air. Instead, they had them down pointed towards the line of police. Then as one, in time with the trucks' speakers, they yelled the last part of the chant.

"And you fall!"

Then they dropped their first and broke into a run towards the barricade. Someone opened fire and the rest followed suit. The energized shields allowed the stun rounds to pass-through and Colleen watched as they hit the line of running figures. They should've all dropped to the pavement and the next volley would take down the now screaming mob standing motionless behind them. But the impacts didn't even slow them down. The rounds hit and their clothing shimmered as the electricity inside them discharged on what could only be energy shields. But that was impossible there was no shielding technology that could be weaved into clothing. If there was, they would have it, but no matter how much they fired the runners never slowed. The officers let their training kick in, the front rank brought up their arm deploying their portable energy shields and setting their feet while the second row aimed guns over their shoulders and fired. This was usually done with sound damping helmets on though and the roar of the gun beside her ear made Colleen scream and close her eyes in pain. When she opened them again the black hooded figures were on them. They leaped into the air impossibly high and cleared the energy shield barricade. They landed in the midst of the riot troops behind the front rank of shields. That is when the chaos truly began.

They carried no weapons, and they engaged the armed and armored officers barehanded. Colleen had just enough time to partially turn to register this before a black-gloved fist hit her in the chest. She was lifted up off her feet and thrown through the air. She hit the energized barricade behind her, and her vision started to fade as her body fell to the ground. She stayed awake long enough to see her fellow officers suffer simpler fates. With every strike, an officer was thrown like a toy. The figures in black were methodical as they tore the riot squad apart. Then everything faded to black.

Captain Rochard Davenport stares at the idea screens inside the command truck. The feeds from the floating drones showed him what was happening, but he could not believe what he was seeing. His officers were being taken apart. Thrown like rag dolls by the blows of these hooded figures. All the while he was shouting orders into the comm, but no one was responding. He wasn't even sure if they could hear him since that damn chanting was still playing over every channel.

"Damn it get me an open line!" he yelled at the officers in the truck with him. They were all with the cyber division and were supposed to be on top of this shit. "Get those Lawbots moving now!"

He didn't listen to their answers as he got back on the comm. He called for the other units that had been kept on standby nearby to move in. But, instead of answers all he heard was that voice.

"Tide! Tide! Tide! We rise!"

"Cut this shit off and clear my fucking comm!"

"Sir, we can't cut it without doing a hard reset on the entire system!"

"God damn it!"

He shoves an officer out of his way and moves back over to another set of screens these dedicated to bodycam feeds. The officer sitting there was staring in stunned silence. Rochard at fifty was not a small man and he worked out religiously. So, bodily pulling the damn fool from his seat and tossing him away did not require a massive amount of effort. He sat in the seat and put his own skills to use. He pulled up the bodycams of S.W.A.T Team Seven who he knew was positioned in an empty building nearby. They were not armed with stun rounds they had live ammunition. He did not know how these assholes had come up with a way to shut off the stunners but the time for nonlethal was over. He had no idea why Sergeant Carver had not already engaged; the man was not exactly known for his patience with these social terrorist groups and their protest. He and his men had practically begged Rochard to add them to riot duty over the last month. So far, they had been responsible for no less than a dozen excessive use of force complaints each, but the word had come down that those were to be ignored and every officer was to be kept on active duty. So, now when extreme force was absolutely necessary where we're they?

He finally got the cameras up and what he saw made his heart sink. All off the bodycams were still and each of them showed the inside of an empty office space. All he saw were the still bodies of Team Seven all of them were laid out and it was impossible to tell if they were alive or dead. One camera moves and Rochard jumped to it. It was Sergeant Carver's feed. All Rochard saw was a black-masked face. He turned on the cameras audio and listened.

"Sergeant Arron Carver, you have been marked for execution by order of The Immortal." A female voice says." You know your crimes so I will not state them. May your soul travel swiftly to its resting place."

Then there was a snap of bone and the view of the camera changed as Arron's body fell to the ground. Rochard stared at the screen in horror and he knew the entirety of Team Seven was dead. Then a new noise made him turn towards the door of the command truck. He looked just in time to see the door being ripped off its hinges and two Lawbots stepped in both of their weapons leveled and sweeping the room. Behind them a hooded figure stepped into the command truck. By the build he knew it was a man. He looked around at all of them before speaking.

"By order of The Immortal you are all under arrest." his voice is loud and commanding. "Do not do anything stupid and-"

One of the officers went for his gun and then one of the Lawbots fired. The three round burst threw the officer off his feet and into a chair where he sat slumped over with a tight three round grouping in his chest.

"As I was saying don't do anything stupid and you won't be harmed." He nods towards the dead officer. "That was an example of stupid. You are prisoners of the Tide now get used to it.

He then looks at Rochard and walks over to him.

"Rochard Davenport, you have been marked for execution by order of The Immortal." the man puts a huge hand around Rochard's throat. "You know your crimes so I will not state them. May your soul travel swiftly to its resting place."

Before Rochard could utter a word, the man gave a sharp twist and his neck snapped.

Victoria watched the scene in utter horror as the police were simply taken apart. The people in black were absolutely brutal. She had never even seen anything like it in real life. They walked through gunfire as if it were rain and moved through the ranks of the police like hunting wolves. All around the members of her group were recording and live streaming the scene.

"No, this is wrong it will only make things worse."

Victoria looks around and sees three figures in black hoodies and mask step of an office building with a for rent sign in the window. Many of the groups rush over to them putting cameras in their faces. The three of them did not push them away or ask them to move they just kept calmly moving forward like a pack of orca knowing they had no natural predators. Victoria rushed over and got in front of the lead figure; it was obvious she was a woman. She and Victoria were the same height and the outfit she wore did nothing to hide her figure. The woman in black stopped and the other two figures did the same.

"You have to stop this; it will not fix anything, only make it worse."

The crowd gathered around them filming and streaming the entire thing.

"We are not here to fix things we are here to change them." the woman in black says." The time for protest and riots is over. The Tide has come to wash it all away and make way for The Immortal to usher in a new world. We are not asking anyone for anything Ms. Vaga, we are here to take it. You feel free to be the voice of peace and acceptance, the world still needs that. But we will be there to defend you against those who want to silence you and show them that if they want war, we will give it to them. Black lives matter and we are no longer asking for justice we are taking it by any means necessary."

All around them the crowd begins to cheer. Victoria is left speechless and the three hooded figures move past her.

"Tide! Tide! Tide! We rise!"

This time it was not a chant it was a war cry, and it was being echoed around the world as it spread like wildfire across the internet.

Tyanna Lucus is a veteran reporter for U.N.N working out of the Atlanta office and in all her years of journalism, she has seen many coups and uprisings throughout the world. As she watched the viral video about this new group known as the Tide, she saw just another radical group that will eventually be put down. They managed to give the Federal Police a nice kick in the nuts, but she knew it could not last long and that it would only end in more useless bloodshed.

Full details of what was happening was, of course, being kept under wraps by the Federal Police but it was quite obvious they were having their asses handed to them. She had gotten the call from her boss Perry Smith to leave her current assignment and get down to Peachtree Street, she had politely refused. Perry could send anybody he wanted but she wasn't leaving one of the most important cases in the history of the city to go give some splinter group some camera time. Tyanna is not political but she is a proud black woman who has ascended to the top of one of the most powerful news networks in the world.

U.N.N came into being after C.N.N bought out nearly every major news network and newspaper in the country after the 2030 stock market crash. This was possible because of the rewriting of Antitrust Laws particularly the one regarding monopolies. So much like the Federal Police Department, U.N.N became pretty much the only game in town. This meant that it could report whatever it wanted and there were few other sources to contradict it. This would normally make the public suspicious and it did, but it also made those who wanted to control news flow furious. U.N.N had a strict no spin policy that made sure their reporters told the story like it was. They never pulled punches or omitted known facts, and this made them a nightmare for people who could once buy the stories they wanted.

Tyanna has reported on stories all over the world but none are more important to her than the ones she reports on regarding the struggles of African Americans. Her current story could not highlight that struggle more. A white supremacist Carl Jennings had walked into a black Baptist Church in Macon, Georgia, and gun down forty-seven black people with an automatic weapon. He then took the time to hang a Confederate flag and was found by police standing in front of the church giving a Nazi salute. When police took him into custody, he admitted everything proudly and was provided with fast food bought by the lead detective. On that same day, an unarmed black teenager was shot and killed for stealing medicine from a convenience store. This was the America they lived in and Tyanna wanted to be the one to expose it. She bit down on this story and held on tight. She had interviewed the family members of the victim and even the shooter. She had interviewed every cop from Macon to Atlanta and had run into the Blue Wall of Silence there. So, she dug into their backgrounds and found out that the arresting officers went to school with Jennings and the detective had been his football coach. This case simply screamed bias and should have been open and shut. But the trial had been dragging on for three days since the defense was going for an insanity plea and had a witness list with no less than seventy names on it. Some experts and others family. The previous day one witness had been a member of the same white supremacist group Carl had belonged to. He proceeded to go into reasons why all the" monkey people" had deserved to die. The judge had actually allowed it until one of the grieving family members charged the witness stand. Of course, it was the family member who was arrested and not the asshole justifying a massacre.

So, while yes, she was only a few miles away from the scene on Peachtree she put her phone away and walked into the courthouse for the third time that week to hopefully see justice served. But her hopes we're not high since in this America a white man killing forty-seven unarmed black people is nowhere near as heinous a crime as a child stealing medicine for his sick mother.

Carl Jennings is walked into the courtroom in shackles and seated in a chair beside his lawyer Mikel Moses. Carl always felt like he needed a shower after sitting next to the Jew, but he had to admit the man was worth every dime the clan had paid him. Just goes to show Jews will do anything for another dime. The lawyer did not even look at Carl and that was fine by him. Carl spun around in his chair and saw many members of the Family of Purity in the audience seats behind him including the group's leader Elijah Wall who had given a spectacular speech in Carl's defense the day before. Of course, the niggers did not agree and one of the monkeys actually attacked Elijah. Carl had enjoyed watching him getting tased and dragged out in cuffs, but he wanted to bleed that darkie for daring to touch Elijah. Carl stands from his seat and throws a Nazi salute to his leader. Every member of the Family of Purity stands and salutes him back. That nearly brought a tear to his eye. Rough hands force him back into his seat. Carl did not fight he had no faith in the justice system knowing it wasn't created for true patriots like himself. But he had no doubt that even if he were found guilty, he would not see a day of prison.

He begins to spin around in his chair like a happy child without a care in the world while he waits. He enjoyed the looks of disgust he received from the niggers, spicks and race traitors in the other audience section. He stopped his spin when he saw the nigger reporter Tyanna Lucus walk in. He had never been with a monkey but if he had to pick one it would be her. She is plump in all the right places but at the same time fit. She always dresses conservatively but it did nothing to hide her assets. He wondered what those fat nigger lips would feel like on his cock. She wore her hair up in braids decorated with silver and gold bands and Carl imagined using them like horse reigns as he plowed her from behind. The thoughts made his dick hard and he gave her a lecherous smile as she looked over at him. Her face turned to one of disgust and she looked away and sat down. She pulls a silver ball from her purse and activates it. The camera drone floats from her hand into the air high enough to give her a good view of the courtroom. Carl just waves up at it and then he hears a door open at the front of the court.

"All rise." the bailiff says. "The Third Federal Court, Criminal Division, is now in session, the Honorable Judge Charles Gaines presiding."

They all stood as the middle-aged judge who had obviously never missed a meal walked in and took his seat.

"Be seated." says the judge and they all did. "First, let me say that nothing like what happened yesterday will be tolerated today. Anyone who disrupts my court will be arrest and held in contempt."

He had barely finished speaking when the doors in the back of the court were flung open with a bang. Carl turned to see what was happening. He saw several figures in black hoodies, masks, cargo pants and boots marching in behind the sharpest looking nigger he had ever seen. The man has dark brown skin and is wearing a pair of designer black shades. His mustache and beard are perfectly groomed, and his black hair is worn in loose dreads that hang past his shoulders. His suit is tailored to fit his obviously heavily muscled frame. He is tall at least 6'4 and radiates an aura of total control that even Carl could not ignore.

"What is the meaning of this?" the judge bellows.

"Greetings and salutations, Judge Gaines." says the man his voice deep and his words pronounced perfectly. "My name is Bryson Kane and I have come here today to make your job just a little easier. Now, if you would kindly remain silent this will not take long."

Judge Gaines turned an unhealthy shade of red and shot to his feet.

"What did you say to me? Arrest all of these people now!"

Every officer in the room pulled their guns and the audience ducked behind seats for cover. Bryson Kane simply raised a hand and snapped his fingers. Several of the hooded figures at his back suddenly burst into movement. They went after the armed officers and the officers opened fire. Carl watched from behind the table and clearly saw as the officer nearest him fired at the hooded figure coming at him multiple times, but the figure did not even slow as the rounds hit. The hoodie simply shimmered and rippled, and the crumpled rounds fell harmlessly to the ground. Then the figure was on the guard and slapped the gun out of his hand. It flew over and landed a few feet from Carl, but he was transfixed. The figure proceeded to take the guard apart with a combo of punches ending it with an elbow to his jaw that dropped the man. All around the courtroom the scene was repeated until everything was silent again. That is when a shadow fell over Carl and he looked up to see Bryson Kane standing over him. The huge man looked over and then bent down picking up the gun that the now unconscious guard had lost. He looked it over a moment and then ejected the clip and checked the load.

"Only one round left, ironic."

He puts the clip back in and takes off his shades. Cold grey eyes meet Carl's green ones. Carl has never known the level of terror he knew in that moment. His bladder released and he pissed his pants.

"Carl Jennings, you have been marked for execution by my order." Bryson says as he lowers the barrel of the gun to Carl's forehead. "You know your crimes so I will not state them. May your soul travel swiftly to its resting place."

"No, wait-" Carl sobbed

Bryson pulled the trigger and blew Carl's hate-filled brain out the back of his head.

Elijah Wall watched as Bryson Kane the richest man alive and CEO of Black Tide executed Carl in front of dozens of witnesses. Before he had come into the courthouse he had watched video of a group of people in hoodies calling themselves the Tide taking out a group of cops at a Black Lives Matter protest, the same group had just taken control of this courtroom as if it were the easiest thing in the world.

He looks over at his wife Abigal Wall and saw that she was feeling under the seat. He knew what she was going for. They had paid one of the court officers to smuggle some guns and other hardware in for them just in case Carl was found guilty. They had planned on taking everyone in the courtroom hostage and using the situation to spread their message, then Elijah and Abigal would escape while the others stayed and become martyrs for the cause. Abigail came up with a handgun and looked over at him, that is when Bryson called his name.

"Elijah Wall, you can stand up now." said Bryson. "You can bring the gun if you like. But I can't promise one of my Black Wolves won't hurt you if you do."

Elijah felt his heart skip a beat. He knew about the weapons, but how? Abigail looks at him, the fear and confusion he felt mirrored in her eyes. He felt a presence over him and looked up and saw one of the Black Wolves standing over him.

"I can promise you that I will hurt you." says the Wolf in a deep voice. "Drop the gun now."

The gun slips from Abigal's trembling hand. The Wolf grabs Elijah by the back of his neck in a grip like a vice. He drags the white supremacist out of his seat and to the front of the court. He deposits Elijah at Bryson's feet.

"Calm yourself, Craig, I am sure Mr. Wall was just taking a moment to compose himself." Bryson offers Elijah his hand. "I apologize for my man's rough treatment Mr. Wall; my Wolves do not like it when someone takes too long to comply with my wishes."

Elijah stares at the offered hand and then up at Bryson's smiling face.

"I would advise you take his hand before I rip yours off." Craig says.

Elijah hurries and takes Bryson's offered hand and is pulled to his feet.

"There we are, isn't that better?" Bryson pats Elijah's shoulder as if they were friends. "So, I hear you want to share your message with the world. So, I am going to help you out. It just so happens they we have a very respected reporter in the room. Ms. Lucus would you please come up and provide us with your assistance?"

Tyanna raises her head from behind the seat in front of her when she hears her name called. She sees that Bryson Kane is standing with his arm around another man she recognized as Elijah Wall, the leader of the white supremacist group known as the Family of Purity. She had received a lot of hate mail from that group recently. Her eyes drifted to the body of Carl Jennings who sat slumped in his chair. She could not believe that Bryson had just executed him for all to see. She felt someone step up beside her and looked up to see one of the people Bryson had called his Black Wolves standing there.

"Nothing to be afraid of ma'am." the Wolf says in a young male voice as he offers her his hand.

She slowly takes it as she rises to her feet. She looked up and realized her camera was still floating there recording, she had gotten all this on camera. The Wolf walks her to the front of the room where three chairs have been set up. Bryson sits Elijah in one of them before walking over and extending his hand to her.

"Ms. Lucus, I am a big fan of your work and I was pleased to find it would be you who be reporting here today." Bryson gives her a winning smile. "If you would be so kind, I would like you to interview me and Mr. Wall today. That is if you are willing, I will understand if you are not."

She stares at him unable to believe that he was speaking with her as if nothing at all was happening. Like he had not just stormed a courtroom, subdued the guards, and executed a man without a second thought. Now, he stood here asking her to interview him. Whatever this was she had to know more.

"I am willing." Tyanna says. "Do you have a list of questions for me?"

"Oh, God no." Bryson looked genuinely affronted. "Do you think I would disrespect your professionalism like that? No, ask the questions that you want the answers to."

He gestures to the chair sitting in front of the two chairs he and Elijah would be sitting in. She took her seat and Bryson addressed the audience.

"Hello everyone, I would like you all to know that no one here is a hostage. "Byson says in a voice that is commanding without yelling. "If anyone wishes to leave you can at any time. No, harm will come to you. My people have taken over the entire building and they will usher you to the exits. Otherwise, feel free to stay and watch."

With that, he sat down beside Elijah. Tyanna did not look behind her but she did not hear anyone running for the exits. Behind Elijah and Bryson, Judge Gaines sat in stunned silence completely untouched. The Wolves even moved the unconscious guards into empty seats. She looks at Bryson who sits back in his chair and crosses his right leg over his left completely at ease.

"Whenever you are ready Ms. Lucus, I am willing to allow Mr. Wall to go first."

Tyanna nods and calls her camera drone down to her with a gesture. She takes it and changes it from record to live stream. She then shoots a quick message to her producer. After putting her phone away, she looks into the camera.

"Hello, everyone this is Tyanna Lucus reporting live from the Atlanta Federal Courthouse where Black Tide CEO Bryson Kane has just taken over the entire building. He then walked into the courtroom, had the people he calls his Black Wolves take down the court officers, and judging Carl Jennings guilty proceeded to execute him with a gunshot to the head."

She pauses and looks at Bryson to see if he was angered by her narrative of what happened. He still smiled at her and waved for her to continue. She looked back in the camera.

"He is now sitting with white supremacist leader of the Family of Purity group Elijah Wall. Mr. Kane has asked me to interview both him and Mr. Wall today and I have agreed. Mr. Kane has made it clear that anyone who wishes to leave the courtroom is welcome to do so as this is not a hostage situation."

With a gesture, she turns the camera to Elijah.

"Mr. Wall are you willing to stay for this interview?"

The white man looks utterly terrified. She had spoken with Elijah Wall before and he had spoken proudly of his hatred. Even called her a breeder monkey. The man she sat across from now had none of that confidence. Beside Bryson and under the watchful eye of the Black Wolves he will little more than a sweating coward. Tyanna felt horrible about it but she had to admit that seeing him like this brought her immense satisfaction.

"Remember, Mr. Wall this is your time to tell the world why you do what you do." Bryson says looking over at the sweating man.

"Y... yes, I am willing to do the interview." Elijah stammered out the words his voice low and weak. "As long as I have your word that I and my people will be allowed to leave after."

"Of course, your people will be allowed to leave."

Elijah looked visibly relieved but Tyanna felt suddenly apprehensive. She knew she should ask the question but something inside her made her keep quiet. Instead, she asked Elijah one question.

"Mr. Wall, why do hate everyone that is not white?"

Elijah apparently getting some of his courage back spoke loudly and clearly this time.

"That is where you are mistaken but I will try to explain it so that even you can understand. I do not just hate everyone not white. I hate everyone who has forgotten that the white race is the superior race. That if not for us all the mud people, wetbacks, and ching changs would still be rubbing two sticks together in the jungles. We created modern civilization and we fought to claim this country. It is ours yet a pure-blooded white man can't even get a job because the law says a nigger deserves it more and then they have the nerve to cry they don't make enough to support their ten kids. So, they cry to our corrupt government to give them free money. In the meantime, hard-working white Americans have their taxes increased to pay for it all. All the while race traitors get up and cheer them on leaving their own people to wallow in the dirt and suffer. I am a patriot and I hate people like you because I love my country, that white hands built, and I am tired of seeing it dragged down by you people. White power!"

He actually stands up and does a Nazi salute. Behind her, she hears his people yell it back at him and applaud. They were really enjoying this 15 minutes of fame. She thought the wolves would attack again but they stood as still as statues. She looks at Bryson who is still smiling. When Elijah sits down, she speaks again.

"Thank you, Mr. Wall." Tyanna says curtly and gestures turning the camera on Bryson. "Mr. Kane, it is your turn now. My question for you is what is your plan?"

Bryson looks straight into the camera

"My goal is simple I am going to take over the world starting with the United States of America." he says it without a trace of humor. "As we speak my forces are taking over the entire state of Georgia. They are taking down every department of the Federal Police and every military base. It will be mine by nightfall and it is only the first. I do this in the name of equality for black people and I am not afraid to say that. That is my main goal, but in the process, I will bring equality to everyone in the world. It is going to be bloody and not everyone is going to agree with it, but the tide of change has started to roll and there won't be anything that can do to stop it. Right now, I only have my focus on this county, but I will slowly conquer them all. My army is in every nation in the form of men and women of all races. I have already infiltrated every government not only with people but with the products my company has released. Robots, software, microchips and so much more. You bought it all from me even if you did not realize it. I give you this information, so you know what is coming. I have chosen America to be a visual example. But do not think that I am not watching. I know how you think, and I warn you if you decide to retaliate against me by harming the black people currently under your charge, I will protect my race at all cost. Do not make me turn my full attention on you. So, sit back and watch and then decide if you want a war with the Tide or if you want to accept the change. This is not me victimizing or enslaving everyone that is not black. This is me demanding what my people have demanded since the first-time chains were put around their necks: freedom and equality. But my demand comes with a clear threat: if you do not give it then I will take it. For those of you watching and thinking that this means just because you are black you can do whatever you want, you are mistaken. Our race has forgotten what we once were, and the world has taught us that we belong in ghettos and on street corners killing each other with poison and bullets for money. This is going to end and if that means I have to cut out the cancer I will. This is my message to the world; it is time for a change and if you work with me it will be as bloodless as possible but if you stand against me then you will learn the true meaning of war. The Tide is here to wash away the old world and usher in the new. It is not one where black people will be the superior race, but it is one where we will finally be treated as equals no matter where we go."

The room is dead silent and Tyanna could hear her heart pounding in her ears. She could not believe her ears; Bryson Kane had just openly declared war on not only the United States but the entire world in the name of equality. Was this reality? Could everything he said be the truth? Was he really prepared to go that far for the dream an entire race of people have shared for thousands of years? Bryson stands and looks at Elijah who looks so pale Tyanna wondered if his heart had stopped.

"Well, Mr. Wall you spoke your peace and I hope it brought you some satisfaction." Bryson buttons his jacket. "May your soul travel swiftly to its resting place."

"What?" Elijah shot to his feet. "But you gave me your word me and my people could leave."

A Black Wolf stepped behind him and locked an arm around his neck. Elijah started to struggle but Tyanna could tell it was pointless.

"No, I said your people could leave." Bryson puts on his shades. "You have been living on borrowed time for quite a while now. I am sorry you wasted it."

The Black Wolf gives a sharp twist and there is an audible snap of bone. When the Wolf let's go Elijah's body slumps to the floor. There is a scream from behind Tyanna and then a red-haired white woman rushes to the front of the court and falls on the body. Tyanna recognized her as Abigal Wall, Elijah's wife. They had met and she was just as insane as him. But did anyone deserve to see the person they loved executed? Then she realized the camera was still going and when she looked up, she saw that the light on the drone was green meaning they were live. She had just broadcasted a public execution.

"Thank you, for your time Ms. Lucus." Bryson says now standing over her. "If you ever want an exclusive feel free to call me."

He holds out a holographic black card with his name and contact info on it. She takes the card with a shaking hand. Instead of letting go he leans in and whispers in her ear.

"If you need anything just call me."

When he let go of the card and stood up Tyanna found herself fighting the urge to grab on to him and never let go. It wasn't a sexual attraction even though she was turned on. This was something deeper like something that had been buried deep in her DNA that only he could awaken. She knew at that moment that she would follow him to hell and back. Bryson gave her a smile and then walked past her. Behind her she heard the start of a chant that would become the war cry of an entire people.

"Tide! Tide! Tide! We rise!"

Soon Tyanna was on her feet with her fist in the air yelling it as loud as she could.

CHAPTER 2

When I stepped off the elevator into the penthouse at the top of my company building Tide Tower located in downtown Atlanta, I was met by my assistant Zephrah Rogers. She stood there with a tablet in one hand and the other on her hip. She is barely 5'0 but her attitude belongs to someone twice that size. She is dressed as usual in a t-shirt, tights and Nikes. Not the normal attire someone would expect the assistant to the richest man in the world to wear, but Zephrah at twenty-six years old is also one of the deadliest women alive and she is always ready to display that fact. She is the leader of my Elites. They are the leaders within the ranks of the Tide, all of them have travelled and studied under me directly.

"You do not look happy." I say as I walk past her.

"Oh, I am not happy." she falls into step behind me. "Since your little interview, we have had 768 hack attempts on our systems. I just uploaded a virus that will most likely cripple the North Korean government for months and I am about to do the same thing to Russia if they keep trying my patience."

"Well aren't you just a ball of sunshine today." I chuckle as I remove my jacket and toss it to my robot Max in the corner. "Drop a tip to South Korea and Japan. Let them know they are free to do as they like."

Both countries are already under my control and had been for years now. I was not bragging when I said I have men and women of every race loyal to me. I call them the Black Wolves now but like me they have gone by many names over the years. A few loyal followers turned into hundreds of bloodlines and that number grew daily. All of them passed down what has become known as The Immortal Faith. They do not worship me as a god, I have never allowed that, but they all swore loyalty to me. This has been going on for well over six millennia now and now my family numbers in the tens of millions.

How do I keep a network this vast together? The answer to that question is my blood. I gave each of my followers some of my blood. When I said I never had children that was not the total truth. I never had any biological children, but my blood had been shared around the world for millennia. A single drop of it would link people to me for the rest of their lives. When my followers had children, they would have a single drop of blood placed on their tongues. From then on, they would always know me and each other, they became known as the Blooded. Believe it or not I originally only sent out seven ounces of my blood, like me it never ages and the cells inside it keep multiplying to whatever container it is held in. So, it has gone from seven ounces to gallons as it was passed from one generation to the next. Each new recruit brought a new family and now I literally sense a new addition to my family daily. It is not a perfect process the blood only works if administered within twelve hours of birth. Not every member received my blood some just came once they heard of me, they are called the Converted. No, my blood does not give my followers superpowers, nor does it make them immortal, their skills are either passed down through their families or earned through individual effort.

The reason I control South Korea and Japan is because the leaders of both countries are both Blooded. They have also promoted many fellow Wolves to key positions within the government. They were both really test cases that were huge successes. Both of those counties have experienced huge social changes over the last decade and a half because of it.

"I figured you would say that, so I already sent the messages." Zephrah says reading my mind as usual. "Also, the President has declared you a traitor and has labeled Tide a terrorist organization. He is also labeling every business you own as a criminal organization. Took him all of fifteen minutes to make that happen. Possibly the fastest decision he has ever made in office."

I poured myself a glass of juice in the kitchen and walked up the steps to the second floor of the penthouse which served as my office. The place is decorated with treasures and trophies that I have taken over the years. Many of them are considered priceless museum pieces. If anyone from the Smithsonian ever got in here, they may have a stroke. I take a seat behind my huge oak desk, putting my feet up and leaning back in my chair.

"How far is he taking this?"

"Well once he finds out that you are telling the truth about taking complete control of Georgia, I have no doubt that he will declare Georgia an enemy state and send in a full invasion force." Zephrah sits in the chair across from me. "Basically, he is going to try to shove several missiles up your black ass."

"An enemy state." I laugh. "Shit looks like I am bringing back the Confederacy. Looks like they were right the South is rising again. Wonder if we can dig up an old flag."

"Please tell me that you are not serious." Zephrah has a look of disgust on her face. "That thing is fucking hideous."

"Nah, I like the new one better anyway."

I look out my wall window at the Westin Peachtree Plaza. I had recently bought the building and now I watched as a massive solid Black Flag was unfurled down the western side of the building covering most of that side.

"Cry havoc and let slip the dogs of war then, Mr. President." I raise my glass to the flag. "I will be releasing the Wolves."

By the end of the first day, the state of Georgia was mine as I promised. Both the Armed Forces and Federal Police had surrendered before midnight, which was not shocking. They stood no chance against the Black Wolves who appeared from outside and inside their ranks. That along with the fact that most modern law enforcement and military hardware is cybernetic. From guns to body armor to explosives everything used microchips and software which of course meant code. Black Tide as the world's largest and most dynamic technology company and our many subsidiaries were, of course, called to service many of these needs. That is where Code Tide was introduced into the game. It is a virus cooked up by the most brilliant minds in my employ and introduced into every product we sell to governments. It is a back door into the production systems and the ingenious part is that it all looks like normal code until the signal is sent to activate it.

I watched many videos of engagements that would have been blood baths if not for Code Tide. Instead, his Wolves simply deactivated weapons, armor, and vehicles as well as turning all the robots against their former owners leaving their targets with two choices: Surrender or fight with whatever they find that still worked. Against the Black Wolves and their next-generation technology, the smart choice was surrender but it was still those who made a fight of it. I did not lose a single Wolf that day and that made me proud. The loses suffered on the other side although controlled were still higher than I liked. I knew this would not be bloodless only a fool would think otherwise, but he watched as fools still fought a hopeless battle and lead others with them. My Wolves were not heartless killers, but they were warriors with a cause, and they were willing to spill blood for it. When the sun rose the next day, the Black Flag hung and flew all over Georgia.

As you can guess though my warnings were not heeded and all around the world more and more Tide cells were activated automatically in response to attacks on black people. The part about this operation that no one outside of my organization understands is that while yes, I am the head of the family as a whole my people did not need me to guide them by the hand. They all believed in the cause they fought for and understood how it was to be fought. If there is one thing the world could always count on it was the fact that the United States believed in its own superiority. As the world watched the Tide showed the so-called sleeping giant the true meaning of superiority.

CHAPTER 3

President Gerald Deckland stared at the screens that lined the walls of the White House's underground situation room. He was fuming and becoming angrier the longer the day went on. He was watching reports from military and Federal Police forces around Georgia. They were all the same they were being completely overpowered. At exactly 8PM the last military base went quiet. Gerald sat quietly as all around him his advisers were in a complete panic. When that bastard Bryson Kane first made his announcement from the Atlanta Federal Courthouse declaring war on not just America but the world in the name of black equality worldwide, Gerald had taken it as a joke. There was no one in the world that powerful not stupid enough to champion a cause that foolish. They could march and riot to their heart's content but there was no force on earth powerful enough to force change through war against America.

Those thoughts began to crumble when his Secret Service detail had literally broken down the door of the Oval Office and rushed him out. He had witnessed several agents open fire on the BT-98 that had stood in the corner of the office. That is when he realized what was happening. The robots which he had asked to be added to his security detail during his first term as president were all products of Black Tide. His Secret Service Director Zachary Richards ordered that every robot in the White House be destroyed and that key personal be evacuated to the underground levels. The agents had rushed Gerald, his family, and other key personal down to the underground bunker while the White House was secured. The reality of the threat they faced happened when the BT-98s started fighting back.

After the first dozen were destroyed the rest changed from sentry mode to attack mode. Secret Service agents suddenly found themselves facing armed robots who fought back. Within ten minutes thirty agents were down and then instead of pressing the attack, the BT-98s simply powered down leaving only one active. This one dropped its weapons and proceeded to broadcast a message in the voice of Bryson Kane.

"Just know that this is me showing mercy President Deckland. If I wanted it the White House would be mine today. But I don't want it, and this is your chance to reconsider your tactics. You believe my people to be animals and you are considering options such as Sanction 45. Well, I am showing what happens when an animal feels threatened, we lash out. So, remember the time I showed mercy the next time you decide to act. Next time I may decide that I want your head."

Then the robots simply left without any further violence, and they were left to pick up the pieces of the first attack on the White House since the War of 1812. Now, they had lost the entire state of Georgia. How was this happening? They were the most powerful country on the face of the Earth. They had policed the world since World War Two. Tyrants ran for cover and entire nations fell in line at the thought of America turning its might on them. They were not used as examples, they made examples. Deckland's rage finally boiled over and he slams his fist onto the table silencing the room. He stands to his feet and glares at every face.

"I want to know every single detail about Bryson Kane." His voice low and filled with menace. "I want every asset he owns frozen and everyone he employs arrested; I want anyone this traitor has ever spoken to questioned. I am officially declaring Georgia an enemy state and I want plans for an invasion drawn up by midnight. This son of a bitch wants to play Moses, then I will show him what would've happened if the pharaoh had jets and hellfire missiles. As of now, the entire country is under martial law and Sanction 45 is in effect. The Federal Police are now militarized and have to power to use any force necessary. He wants to use us as examples then we will show the world that America is not to be fucked with. Now move!"

The room suddenly was abuzz with new energy. Gerald sat down and took a sip from his water bottle. He watched as his orders were carried out and then he looked at his Chief of Staff Lena Andrews.

"Have a press conference scheduled for in the morning." he runs his hand up her thigh under the table. "Stay available tonight, once Angela is asleep, I will send for you."

"Yes sir, Mr. President." Lena puts her hand on his and gives him that beautiful smile.

They had been lovers for years and her being his Chief of Staff meant no one looked twice when they spent hours alone together. His wife Angela had her head so far in the clouds she would barely notice if he brought in a street hooker. They hadn't had sex in six months, and he did not mind if they didn't for another six. Angela was a prude and barely let him touch her even during sex. Lena, on the other hand, did things to and for him that would make porn stars blush. When she had been brought down to the bunker along with their two children, she had actually complained about missing her nail appointment. He was stressed and he needed the release only Lena could give him. When she got up and went to make phone calls, he couldn't help but stare at her perfect ass.

When he finally looked away, he saw his Vice President Frank March looking at him. Frank is one of the few who knew about the affair.

Frank gives Gerald a knowing smile, "I can cover for you. You can lead better if your mind is clear."

Gerald returns his friend's smile and then gets up. He whispers to a Secret Service agent to bring Lena to the underground Oval Office and then he leaves the situation room followed by agents. Gerald walks into the underground Oval Office and barely has time to pour himself a drink when Lena came in. The door had barely closed behind her before the forty-five-year-old Puerto Rican Chief of Staff was kissing him. He drops his drink and gives her his full attention. She undid the buttons of his suit and shirt with nimble fingers. Her hands felt like electricity when she put them inside his shirt and started to caress his body. She starts to kiss her way down his body as she goes slowly to her knees. When she is at eye level with his crotch she looks up and her hazel eyes shine with wicked intent. Gerald is so lost in her eyes that he doesn't realize she has undone his belt and his pants and underwear are around his ankles. Lena takes his hard cock in her hand and starts to massage it earning a moan of pleasure from Gerald.

"We cannot have you stressed at your press conference, Mr. President." Lena says with a wicked grin. "Let me help you relax."

Gerald's eyes damn near roll into the back of his head as she takes him into her warm mouth. His wife never gave him head and if she did it would not even come close to what Lena was doing to him.

She deep throats him, and Gerald screams as he nuts, "God, bless America!"

Gavin Hopper president of Ebony Unlimited sits in the conference room on the top floor of the company headquarters in New York City. He watches the television as the President of the United States addresses the county. The news that Georgia had fallen the day before had rocked not only the nation but the world. It was the leading story on every major news network around the globe. After all The Immortal had clearly told them they were next.

Gavin is a Blooded and an Elite, his entire family are followers of The Immortal Faith and now it was finally time for them to share it with the world. All around the conference room stood other Wolves all of them in the black hoodies, cargo pants, black boots, black masks and black Force-Gloves that are the uniform of the standard Black Wolf warrior. The technology inside the simple clothing is next generation. The clothing is made out of a light, but tough material called synth-wear. It was developed and patented by one of the many companies owned by The Immortal over a decade earlier. The technology inside the clothing was also created by one of his companies like the nano shield generators and exo-weave but neither was ever released to the public. These were kept secret and incorporated along with many other advancements into the armament of the Black Wolves. The Force-Gloves are their main weapons, and they work just as the name suggested. When a Wolf strikes a target there is a blast of force that hits the target. The level of impact can be adjusted from low to bone-crushing. The black mask they all wore lets them communicate privately with each other, control their systems and most importantly they unite them by giving them all one identity.

Gavin is in a set of black form fitting armor that only the Elites are given. His armor is meant to allow him to run operations across an entire state without having to be trapped inside a command center and make the Elites lethal game changers in any fight. It allows him to fly with the Gen One Grav-Jet flight system. His combat capabilities are increased to an inhuman level, the shield systems are even more powerful than those of the standard combat uniform and it comes with a variety of weapons systems. He is not currently wearing a retractable helmet and faceplate as he watches the President's broadcast.

"So, I am declaring martial law effective immediately as well as activating Sanction 45 which temporarily suspends all Constitutional and Civil rights of American citizens. The Federal Police Force along with the military will be taking full control of all U.S cities and towns. They will have the authority to requisition any resources they deem necessary and conscript anyone into service. They will also be able to search private property and make arrests without warrants. Anyone who resists will be declared enemies of the state and will be treated as such. These measures may seem extreme, but they will remain in place until the terrorist threat known as the Tide is neutralized. I am declaring their leader Bryson Kane public enemy number one and issuing a reward of five million dollars for information that leads to his capture or termination. Black Tide and all of its subsidiary companies within the United States and its territories are declared terrorist assets. They will be raided; they will have their assets seized and all employees will be arrested and questioned. The state of Georgia is hereby declared an enemy state. It will not be considered as part of the United States until it is retaken. We will not be terrorized, and we will not fall to tyranny. The United States is the greatest country on Earth, and we will show the world our strength. Stand with me my fellow Americans and let's make America great again. God bless you loyal Americans and God bless America."

The broadcast ended and the room was silent.

"Did he just turn America into Nazi Germany?" someone asked from behind Gavin.

"America has been Nazi Germany for decades." Gavin says. "He just stopped lying about it."

There is a beep from his left gauntlet, he pulls up the holographic screen with a tap and he checks the message.

"Police have started their raids. You are a priority target. You are free to engage."

He puts the phone down and stands up. He looks around the room at the faces of his brothers and sisters. There was a representative of nearly every race and nationality there. His eyes met those of his wife of fifteen years Keira, and they took each other's hand for a moment. Then his helmet and faceplate form over his head and face. Everyone in the room dons their mask making themselves combat ready.

"The Immortal has unleashed us." his voice is now cold and machine like as it comes from his armors speakers. "But we do not fight for him. We fight for everyone who has ever cried for freedom and equality. We fight for those who were slaughtered just because of the color of their skin. I am a proud black man and I thank you all for standing behind me as I fight to prove that my life and the lives of my people matter. As you fight for us, we will fight for you and together we will become the tide of change. Now, it is time for us to prove we are willing to fight, kill, and die for that change."

Fists are raised and the war cry fills the room.

"Tide! Tide! Tide! We rise!"

Cars and trucks belonging to the New York division of the Federal Police surround the headquarters of Ebony Unlimited. The back of one of the trucks open and Sergeant Gage Robertson team leader of S.W.A.T Team Twelve leaps out. He is quickly followed by the rest of his team. They quickly moved to stack up on the eastern entrance to the building with about twenty regular officers as back up.

"Sharp, get a sonic charge on the door." Gage says into his team comm.

S.W.A.T Officer Clyde Sharp moved up and put a sonic breathing charge on the glass door and then gave Gage a thumbs up.

"Team Twelve in position and ready to breach." Gage says into the general comm channel shared by everyone on the raid.

"Acknowledged." came the voice of Captain Annette Tucker.

Gage slowed his breathing and steadied his thoughts. He did not have a good feeling about this. Like everyone else in the world, he had spent yesterday watching the videos coming out of Georgia. He had listened to Bryson Kane's message and witnessed the hell he was ready to unleash in order to realize his goals. He is a white man married to a black woman and he had seen the look on his wife's face as they watched Kane's broadcast. He could only describe it as satisfaction.

His relationship with Belinda had never been affected by race. They loved each other's families and liked each other friends. They lived in a nice neighborhood that was predominantly white and there had never been any issues that he knew of. But last night something seemed to change and this morning after the President's address she gave him a look she had never given him before as he walked out in his uniform, it was disgust. She had walked past him without a word and locked herself in their bedroom. He had stood at the door for almost half an hour knocking and trying to explain to her that he was only going to do his job. That the Sanction was not aimed towards black people it was meant to give them the ability to protect the country during a crisis. His words had been answered with silence.

He finally gave up and left for work. The whole drive there he listened to people comparing them to the Gestapo and the President to Hitler. At first, he was angry, and then he was horrified. Was that what Belinda saw when she looked at him? Did she see a Nazi? They had been together since they were in high school in Rhode Island and they had three beautiful kids together. He had never disrespected her, her family, or her race. So, how could she see him like that?

Gage pushed the thoughts to the back of his mind and focused on the task at hand. No matter what he had to do this job, he had sworn an oath to defend America, and right now the Tide is the greatest threat to America.

"All teams go."

The order came and Gage nodded to Clyde. Clyde activated the charge, and a high-pitched wail was emitted. The thick glass shattered, and Gage was the first in.

"S.W.A.T!" he yelled and as he tracked his weapon side to side.

He heard his team yelling the same thing behind him and the other S.W.A.T teams as well as they entered the lobby from all sides. The place was completely empty though. They fanned out and secured it completely checking every office, closet, and bathroom before declaring it clear. Each team has radioed it in and waited as sixty other officers entered the building led by Captain Tucker.

"Alright everyone listen up." the Captain says getting everyone's attention. "I know that many of you are not comfortable with the current situation. But today no one is black, white, Asian, Latino or any other race except blue. We are the law, and we have our orders. We don't have to like them but for the good of America, we have to follow them. Now, you all know what to do. Arrest anyone you find to be brought in for questioning and seize any electronic devices? Any computers you come across you plug in one of these remote access USBs."

She holds up one of the USBs everyone there is carrying and then walks behind the front desk and plugs it into the computer there, it turns green and beeps.

"Simple, each of you has your assigned teams let's get this done people."

Gage leads his team and the officers that followed them to the eastern staircase. Each group had been given floors to clear in the 30-floor building, Gage leads his group to the third floor.

"Team Twelve entering the third floor." Gage says in over the general comm.

Team Twelve entered first to clear and secure. Just like the lobby, the floor was completely empty. This added to the uncomfortable feeling Gage had. He gave the all-clear and the other officers came on and started the search and seize process. Desks were broken open and USBs were put into computers. It took about ten minutes before they were ready to move again. They moved up to the sixth floor which was once again empty and repeated the process. This continued until they got to the fifteenth floor, that is when the comms went out.

"Team Twelve entering the fifteenth floor." Gage said into the comm.

This time all he got was static.

"12-1 to command do you copy?"

All he got was static, he switched to the team channel.

"Comm check."

Still, he got nothing but static. He opens his helmet and motions for his team to do the same.

"Are any of your comms working?"

The entire team checks and answers in the negative. They have the other officers do the same and all of theirs are down as well.

"Shit, we are being jammed that is the only explanation." says Gage." Alright everyone heads up we are most likely about to be engaged. Remember these people are highly dangerous. No one is to fire until I give the order, clear?"

Everyone gives him an affirmative. Gage ejects his mag and checks the load. He sees the green tips of the anti-shield rounds. They had all been issued with them to counter the shield technology used by the Black Wolves. As far as he knew no one had tried these against them yet, but they were specifically made to pierce energy shields. He puts his face plate back down and puts the clip back in nodding to Clyde who is waiting with his hand on the door. Clyde opens it and Gage leads Team Twelve in. He freezes as he sees five hooded

Black Wolves waiting for them. They are all relaxed either sitting on desk or leaning back in chairs with their boots on the desk. One is even playing on a cell one, it is that one that looks up and speaks.

"Damn, it took you long enough." the voice is female and utterly unbothered.

She takes her feet off her desk and stands up pocketing the phone. Gage snaps his aim to her.

"S.W.A.T, by order of the President of the United States you are all charged with treason and terrorism!" his voice is amplified by his helmets external speakers. "Get down on your knees and place your hands behind your head, you are under arrest!"

"Oh, that's a negative ghost rider." the woman says with obvious amusement." The only time I kneel before a man is when I am servicing my husband and you aren't him. So, why don't you put down that gun and get on your knee before you get hurt?"

"This is your final warning." his grip tightening on his gun and his finger entering the trigger guard." Get on the ground or we will open fire."

A second Black Wolf steps up behind the first one. This one is taller and when he speaks the voice is male.

"That is not a good idea." says the second Wolf." This doesn't have to turn to violence. You can just surrender, and we will take you all prisoner. You will be treated fairly and when the time is right you will be sent home to your families. Just put down your weapons and we can end this."

"Fire!"

He pulls his trigger, and his gun clicks. He pulls it again and it clicks again. All around him the guns of his team do the same thing. Gage looks at the status display in the side of his weapon and sees a lock symbol there. He flicks the electronic safety on and off, but the lock remains there. He looks back at the Wolves and sees they are all on their feet now.

"Very well." the male Wolf says, his voice heavy with disappointment.

"Some people can only learn by example, Howard." the female Wolf cracks her knuckles. "You can make the offer again after we show them what option B looks like."

Before Gage can say another word, the female Wolf attacked. She was so fast she covered the twenty feet between them in seconds. Gage felt the blow to his gut and that sent him up through the ceiling tiles. He was unconscious before he hit the floor again. He would only hear about what happened next.

The five Wolves took his team apart. Amazingly they all survived the brutality. Then they gave the other officers the same offer. Seeing what happened to the S.W.A.T team had the desired effect all, but a few, surrendered peacefully. Those who didn't were also made examples of. This happened to the other team and groups as well, not everyone was lucky enough to survive. Captain Tucker had been executed outright for crimes apparently only The Immortal and the Wolves knew about. But Gage would only learn about this when he woke up. As a prisoner, he would watch in horror and amazement as the Wolves rose and took the state of New York unleashing the true might of the Tide on any who stood against them.

Adrianna Ballard is a single mother who works two jobs to support her family. Her mother Lottie Ballard has lung cancer and over the years her condition has deteriorated to the point that it was no longer possible to live on her own. Adrianna had to move her into her rent-controlled three-bedroom apartment in the Chicago area known as West Englewood. The neighborhood had never been considered safe with at least three different gangs calling it home. It wasn't the ideal place to try to raise two teenagers especially since she worked six days a week only taking Sunday off both her jobs so that she could take her children to church.

With her mother being moved in she was worried about the strain that would add with medical cost, the specialized care she needed, and the lack of space. She had to move Mailya and Chris into the same room and then move into Chris' old room so that her mother could have hers which was the biggest. She was so relieved when she found out that the company her mother retired from Black Tide still allowed her to keep her insurance which was amazing. Not only did it completely cover the cost of her medicine and treatment it also provided her with a robotic nurse. The robot which the kids had affectionately named Auntie quickly became another member of the family. She has a female personality and while her primary job was to care for Lottie she did so much more. She took care of household chores, helped the kids with their homework, and even cooked. Suddenly, Adrianna's world did not feel so chaotic. Then she watched the President's address, where he not only declared martial law but enacted a sanction, she had never heard off that stripped every American of their rights.

"Yeah every American except the rich white one." Mailya said.

Adrianna could not argue with her daughter. It was scary enough being black when they had rights only to have them violated on a regular basis. Now, the police could do whatever they wanted to whomever they wanted. She had heard Bryson Kane's message but when it came to promises from black men, she has little to no faith. So, she did all she could to make sure they were safe.

With martial law in place, it was no way she was going into work or out to the store. She went online and she found that drone delivery was still available, so she placed an order for groceries and asked Auntie to go out on the balcony to receive it which she did without complaint. Their apartment was located on the third floor on the west side of the building and the only area with a view anywhere near the front of it is the master bedroom where Lottie is currently sleeping. So, no one has any idea that the Gang and Vice Unit of the Chicago Federal Police are using their newfound power to crack down on gangs they have been going in circles with for years.

Adrianna is in the kitchen washing dishes when the sound of her door being broken down makes her jump. She runs to her living room where her kids are as raised voices echo through the house.

"Get on the fucking ground now!"

Adrianna runs in and sees both of her kids are on their knees with two police officers pointing guns in their faces. The black officer sees her and turns his gun on her.

"Get face down on the ground now!" he yells.

Adrianna looks over and sees that Mailya is crying while Chris is glaring at the officers with hatred in his eyes.

"Officer please they are just children." Adrianna says gesturing to her children. "They-"

"I said get on the ground now I will not ask a third time." the black cop advances on her.

"Leave my mother alone!" Chris yells from the floor.

The white cop holding the gun on him steps forward and kicks him in the gut. Chris doubles over in pain and the cop stands over him with his gun aimed at the back of Chris' head.

"You don't tell us what to do you little banger piece of shit." he places the barrel of his pistol directly on Chris' head. "Why don't I just do the world a favor and end you now."

"No, please I am begging you." Adrianna fell to her knees. "He isn't in a gang he has never hurt anyone in his life. Officer, please have mercy."

The white cop looks over at her and gives her a smile that Adrianna can only describe as evil.

"Hmm, well I say he is a banger and now I am wondering what you are willing to do to change my mind." his eyes drift down to her breast. "Why don't you let me see what is under that shirt? Looks like you are sporting quite a pair."

"Mama, please don't." Chris pleads as he regains his breath.

The officer pushes his gun into the back of his head harder.

"If she doesn't, I will be blowing your worthless brains all over the nice carpet." the white cop growls. "So, if I were you, I would shut the fuck up."

Adrianna looks up at the black cop holding his gun on her. Hoping to see some form of compassion in his eyes at seeing people the same color as him being terrorized. But all she saw was lust in his eyes as he eyed her breast as well. Adrianna had lost faith and hope in the myth that black men were meant to be protectors and providers years ago after her husband walked out of their lives. This moment hammered that fact home for her. No one was coming to save her or her children only she could do that. So, with shaking hands she pulled her shirt over her head dropped it on the floor. She wore no bra, so her breasts were completely exposed to them. She felt tears sting her eyes as she heard them wolf whistle, but relief washed over her as the white cop removed the gun from Chris's head as he walked towards her.

"Now we are going to have some-" the white cop started but at that moment the ceiling over him collapsed.

The cop disappeared under a cloud of white dust everyone else fell away coughing. Adrianna looks up in time to see a hand take the black cop by the throat and lift him up off the ground. The other hand breaks his wrist making him drop his gun. The man would have screamed but Adrianna doubted he could breathe as Auntie held him there with his feet dangling off the ground. Then she twisted and the man's neck snapped audibly. The robot dropped the body on the floor and then turned her glowing red eyes on Adrianna. After a moment, the eyes went from red to their normal green.

"I apologize, Adrianna, I did not mean for you to have to suffer like that." Auntie said, in her robotic voice calm." But I needed this one to take his gun off of Chris before I could engage."

She gestures at the white cop who lays dead, crushed under her feet. Adrianna hurries to put her shirt on and rushes over to both her kids. She pulls them both to her, they hugged her tightly and all three of them cried. Auntie simply collected the two officers' weapons and ammunition.

"In accordance with Code Tide directives I am now switching to combat mode in order to protect you." Auntie checks the weapons. "I will protect this floor against any forces deemed a danger. Please remain in the apartment while this is happening. I suggest the master bedroom, stay low, and close the door. Please adjust Ms. Lottie's bed to its lowest setting."

Auntie moved to the destroyed door now armed for combat.

"Auntie wait." Chris says and the robot turns to him. "I thought you could not hurt humans. Who is telling you to do this?"

"My original programming did not allow me to hurt humans." Auntie says. "But I am now operating under the directives of Code Tide. These directives have been handed down by Bryson Kane. I will do what I must to protect the innocent. Please remain inside."

With that she stepped out into the hallway. Soon they hear gun fire from down the hallway followed by Auntie's voice giving others the same order to stay in their apartments.

"I told you it was real mom." Chris hugs his mother and pulls his sobbing sister close. "They really are here to fight for us."

Adrianna hugged him tighter and kissed his head. She looked at the dead cops and found that she felt no pity for them. All the church in the world could not make her forgive what these men had done to her family. She found herself hoping that Auntie killed them all. She also found a renewed faith not in all black men but in Bryson Kane. He not only spoke of change he was delivering it. She held her babies and thanked God for sparing their lives.

Colleen Johnson has had her life turned upside down in a single week. When she woke up from the attack on the barricade, she found herself stripped out of her riot gear with her hands zip-tied behind her back. She was sitting up against the side of a building beside other cops all also stripped down to their uniforms and zip tied. All around them black hooded figures, who she would later find out are known as Black Wolves and Lawbots, stood protecting them as a crowd of people jeered and booed them while they took pictures and videos. Some even attempted to throw things at them but much to her surprise the Black Wolves and Lawbots did not allow that.

The transport vehicles that they had brought with them to take in prisoners were used instead to transport them back to their precinct where they found more Black Wolves and Lawbots in control. They all had their ties cut and were told that they would be held there as prisoners and as long as no one caused any trouble they would not be harmed. Of course, some of the officers did not listen and the Black Wolves made examples of them. After that, there was no more trouble as the rest understood they had no chance of overpowering the high-tech terrorist. Colleen found Luke as soon as possible and they stuck together. They were given food, water and medical care. They were even given phones to call their families and to entertain themselves.

On day three they were all released, and Colleen found Eli waiting for her with their two kids Shane and Bianca in the backseat and as much as their lives as possible packed in the trunk. Luke's wife Dora was also there, and they all headed straight for the Georgia/Alabama Stateline. When they got there, they found cars backed up for miles since the military under orders from the President had blocked anyone from leaving the state. Colleen understood that strategy. He did not want the Black Wolves to escape and spread but by this time New York and at least five other states had already been taken. They were trying to figure out what they were going to do when the military opened fire on the front of the line. They literally killed dozens who were only trying to get out of the state that had basically been excommunicated from the country.

Colleen and Luke both got back in their cars and got their families out of there. For the first time in her adult life Colleen had felt her faith in America shaken to it's very core as she drove back to Atlanta. They get back into the city and decide that everyone will be staying in Johnson's three-bedroom apartment. The Harps have no kids, so it is an easy enough fit. Colleen sends the kids to their rooms while her, Like, Eli and Dora sit and try to plan their next move.

"I can't believe they just opened fire on those people." Eli says

They had heard the shots and bolted but were too far back to actually see what happened. On the ride back Eli had pulled up the U.N.N app on his phone. They had reporters stationed near the area and they caught the entire thing on camera. The military had roadblocks set up at the Stateline, fences backed by vehicles and troops. People were at the fence demanding to be allowed through. A military officer was standing on the back of a truck telling them all they would not be able to cross into the United States due to them being considered possible enemy combatants. That is when things got out of hand as people started shouting about their rights being violated and how they were tax-paying Americans. They had all seemed to forget that Sanction 45 was in effect or they just did not believe it applied to them. Then a white man walked away from the fence and climbed into a semi. He started it and hit the gas gunning it for the fence. He ran people down who were not fast enough to get out of his way. That is when the military opened fire using weapons meant for war to destroy the truck and kill its driver. If they had stopped there maybe people would've understood but they kept firing into the crowd, and it became a wholesale slaughter that had already earned the title the Stateline Slaughter.

Seeing it had turned Colleen's blood to slush. She could not justify what she had seen. She couldn't say it was doctored as many no doubt would. She had heard the shots, and no-one could doctor footage that fast. They had massacred people who had only been looking for their protection.

"Maybe, it was the Black Wolves." Luke says. "Maybe that guy was one of them like a suicide bomber. I mean they are terrorist causing chaos and turning people against the government is what they do."

Colleen looks at her partner she sees that even he doesn't believe that. They had been among the Wolves for days and unless provoked they were not violent. This was not their doing and as much as she wanted to, she could not blame them. Driving in she had seen the food trucks, shelters, and mobile clinics. They were helping people while the government was turning guns on them. She knew their hands had blood on them, but from what she saw they did not engage in violence just to do it. She had also heard about the executions for crimes that apparently only they knew off. She had feared she would be on that list but here she was alive and free.

"We need to go get food and supplies." Colleen finally said looking at Eli. "You and Dora stay here babe. Luke and I will go."

"Are you sure?" asked Eli. "I can help love."
She kisses her husband and puts her head against his. They stay like that for a while before she leans back.

She whispers to him, "I love you so much babe, I know you can help but I need you here with our kids. If anything happens to me, you are all they have."

Eli nods and kisses his wife. He is a brave man and she had been teaching him to fight and shoot but, in the end, he is an accountant. He grew up a sheltered black kid in the suburbs who never had a fight in his life. She knew he loved her, and he would die to protect her and her family, but she would do anything to keep that from happening.

"We will be back my love." she stands up.

"Where do you keep your guns?" Luke asked after kissing Dora.

"We can't go armed Luke this is their city and their rules." Colleen meets his eyes.

They had been warned before they were released to keep their weapons at home in the streets they were not to be armed. Luke looks ready to argue but he just nods.

"We will be back keep the door locked."

They leave and head downstairs. They are passing an open apartment door when Luke takes her arm and guides her in. The place is quiet, and he closes and locks the door. He turns as looks at her and then he presses her against the wall and starts to kiss her. This part of the relationship had been going on for months, but they had agreed to let it go. That was until all this shit started. Those three days stuck together as prisoners had rekindled the passion. Colleen kissed him back as they started to undo each other clothes. He got her belt loose and turned her around pushing her up against the wall. He pushes her pants and panties down and few seconds later she let out a moan of pleasure as he slides his cock inside her. She was dripping wet and he did not have to work hard. He pressed his body against hers's and their fingers interlocked as he made love to her right there. She moaned in pleasure, but tears of shame rolled down her cheeks as she thought about Eli. She truly loved him, and she was doing this literally right under his nose. But at that moment she needed the love and passion only Luke could provide. She gave herself to him until they both let out screams of pure ecstasy as they came together.

CHAPTER 4

I watched as Tide spread with little to no help from me. My people simply reacted when it was called for just as I said they would, not only in America but around the world. Major cities and entire states fell one after the other. They did not heed my warning and they paid for it dearly as the Black Flags were raised. They thought that this was finally their time to show their true colors only to find out that the Tide was not an army at their gates it was an assassin's blade at their throats. I watched from my tower as more and more territory was added until finally my point was made. President Deckland quietly issued orders to the Federal Police and military to stop their raids. Instead he focused his attention on me specifically. Around the world, other governments also ceased their activities and they started to take a closer look at me and how I fought this war.

I had already moved to the next stage of my operation. While my Wolves fought, I started to reform. I began in Georgia. The first thing I did was release the members whose jobs weren't to fight but to build and heal. This started with fleets of mobile hospitals and food trucks. They spread all across the state calling for the sick and hungry to come. Prefab shelters were built to get the homeless off the streets. They were given food, water, medicine, and just shown basic human kindness. The doors of the hospitals were thrown open to admit those who needed more advanced care without anyone being turned away because they could not pay. I did not just watch all of this from my tower I got out in the streets and walked the homeless to shelter and even did my part to care for the sick. My favorite part was seeing the smiles on faces as they felt like they mattered again.

There were those who did not want any part of my vision. I have to say I have never laughed as hard as I did when the I saw a group of armed KKK members attempt to start an armed march on my tower chanting "White Lives Matter" and firing guns into the air. You can guess how that ended. After that, I made it known that no one was being forced to stay. The Federal Police and military personal that had been taken prisoner during the takeover had been released back to their families and anyone was free to pack up and leave. But if they stayed then they could either peacefully fend for themselves or change their attitudes and accept the way things worked now. Many did pack their vehicles and head out of state only to find themselves being arrested or even attacked by the military forces that had been stationed at the state lines. Some of them managed to turn around and escape back into Georgia.

The military learned early that Georgia was a no-go zone. Three days after my take over they had attempted to start the invasion by sending in a squadron of jets to make an attack run on Atlanta. As soon as they crossed into Georgia airspace my people remotely took control of the jets and landed them at the nearest airport where Wolves were waiting to take the pilots captive. The next attempt was a navel assault with the Forth Fleet. As soon as the fleet came within range, I warned them that if they followed the President's orders to fire missiles at Atlanta that I would show them no mercy. They did not listen so when they tried to fire the missiles simply self-destructed. Five ships including state of the art Titan-class battleship the USS Gloryheart were badly damaged. Even though I said I wouldn't, I had shown some mercy by ordering that the explosive yield of the missiles be dialed down. Call me a softie if you like but I really did not want to repaint the world red, just prove that if pushed I would do what I had to do.

I then had my people take control of the ships and park them just off the coast of Georgia. Where they are currently still sitting fully crewed. I have issued terms of surrender to each captain individually. But so far none have accepted. Though many of the sailors have started jumping overboard and swimming to shore where they surrender themselves to the Wolves waiting there.

Seeming to have learned his lesson President Deckland has not tried a land invasion yet preferring to station troops at each of the state lines. I think he is planning to starve us out. I am fine with letting him try, no use taking the stick from a monkey if he is doing no harm.

I am standing in the inside of the newly built shelters watching as people are given food, offered showers, and given fresh clothes. No one is forced to stay and many leave not trusting the kindness they are being shown. Those that do are given enough food and water to last a few days along with a few changes of clothes and hygiene supplies. They are told they are welcome back at any time and then they are allowed to leave. Kindness is freely shown and should be freely accepted not forced. So, my people will continue to show kindness and one day the world will learn to accept it without worrying that they will regret it later.

There is a tap on my arm, and I turn to see Tyanna Lucus standing there. The woman is wearing a white t-shirt, black pants, and a pair of Nike's. Her hair is up in a ponytail and she is wearing a broad beautiful smile as she looks up at me.

"I think this is the first time I have seen you out of a suit."

I am currently wearing a black shirt, pants, and boots with my usual black shades.

"A suit isn't appropriate for every occasion." I say. "What brings you out here? Doesn't seem like you are working."

"Morning exercise, my apartment is a few blocks away." she looks around. "You know I expected you to be flanked by guards. I have seen very few Black Wolves considering their leader is here."

"I don't travel with any bodyguards." I gesture around the shelter . "Actually, many of the people you see here are Black Wolves, the title is not reserved for those that fight. The warriors you have seen are only here to guard against troublemakers. Not everyone is happy with the new way of things, but I only travel with an escort if I am specifically looking for trouble."

"You are trying to break every mold, aren't you?"

"Yes I am." I say without a seconds hesitation. "Society putting people in molds is what is wrong with the world today. I am trying to show everyone that no one is better than anyone else. That given an equal chance anyone can bring change to the world. I understand the need for order, and I am not denying the fact that at the end of this I will be in charge. But, as a leader, I will break yet another mold by actually giving a damn about my people. All of them, not just the ones who the world has deemed the elite. Some will call me a dictator and tyrant, I am fine with those titles as long as I can spread freedom and equality to every man, woman, and child. Some will say I have no right to do this, I say I do because I took that right. The world was built by the strong dominating the weak. Now, I am taking it from the strong and showing those deemed weak that given a fair chance that they possess more strength than they ever imagined. Black people are the most hated and abused race of people on this planet. Simply because we were put in chains and unlike every other race we didn't rise up and say enough. We meekly marched, silently prayed, and loudly begged to just be allowed to use an indoor bathroom or eat decent food. But, after all that, instead of freedom we got tolerance. We are tolerated as long as we stay in our proper place and don't complain. That is the state we have been in since slavery was abolished across the world. Yet we are still treated like slaves, the chains are just harder to see. You can go anywhere in the world and see black people suffering at the hands of Caucasians, Asians, Latinos, East Indians, Arabs, and even other black people. We aren't even welcome in

Africa the place of our birth. We have to claim a color because we have no home."

I stopped myself then as I saw the tears in not only her eyes but the eyes of everyone around me. I realized that my voice had risen, and I was no longer having a conversation but giving a speech. I look up and see the camera drone hovering above recording me. I don't remember seeing her deploy that. I close my eyes and take a deep breath to calm myself, then I look at her again.

"I have seen the pain of oppression." my voice is back down to conversational tones. "I will not allow it to continue. I fight for equality not only to free my people but all peoples who have had to live under the boot of those deemed better because of the color of their skin or the size of their bank accounts."

I finish the impromptu interview with a smile, and it is greeted with applause from everyone there including Tyanna. I accept them with a nod as I silently kick myself for letting my emotions get the better of me. Nothing I said was a lie, but I hated losing control of myself like that. With a gesture, Tyanna called the drone down and then looked at me like a hopeful student.

"I only recorded." she said softly. "I will delete it if you want me too."

"No need." I am still smiling. "Send it in for broadcast, I only request that it not be edited."

"You have my word.".

"Also, do you have any dinner plans?"

The expression on her face at my question is one of comical surprise.

"N...no I don't."

"How does 8 o'clock sound?"

CHAPTER 5

Victoria Vaga was so confused as she sat in her usual spot in the choir stand of her father's church Saint Mark Baptist Church. Her father Pastor Noah Vaga was in the pulpit preaching a sermon on how man believed they could do God's work on their own. The church consisted of a mixture of people, but it was majority black, and Victoria was surprised to see that so many people were in attendance. It had been a full week since Bryson Kane and his Tide took over the city. His most recent speech was being played over and over on U.N.N. His words hit home with many people and Victoria was one of them. She had always been taught to wait for God to move but here was a man who had stood up to fight and was not only winning but changing the way the world worked. Her father did not see it that way and he had preached himself into a fever pitch

"I tell you, brothers and sisters, God is not pleased." Pastor Vaga yells into the mic. "He says in his word that vengeance is his and that the meek will inherit the earth. Taking matters into our own hands is not the way, shedding the blood of our fellow man is not the way and following in the footsteps of false prophets is not the way. This is a sign of the end of days my brothers and sister. Revelation 20:10: And the devil that deceived them was cast into the lake of fire and brimstone, where the beast and the false prophet [are] and shall be tormented day and night for ever and ever. This will be the fate of all false prophets, do not follow them down that path to damnation."

Many of the older members we're on their feet clapping and shouting but Victoria saw that many of the younger members were still in their seats. Then she saw Jermaine Stokes a guy she went to school with walking up the center aisle. It was what he was wearing that caught her attention: a black hoodie, jeans, and boots. He walked right up to the alter and stared up at her father who finally noticed him.

"Brother Stokes?"

The church went quiet as everyone noticed him.

"Who are you to judge?" Jermaine asked." Who are any of you to judge? What have you ever done to help our race get up off its knees? All you do is speak pretty words from a book written by white men. How do we even know those are the words of God when it has King James on the side of it?"

"That is enough!" says Deacon Vernon English stepping toward Jermaine.

Jermaine looks at the older man.

"Try Jesus not me Deacon, because I will bend your shit if you touch me." the tone in the young man's voice promised violence.

Victoria watched as her father waved the deacon off and then addressed Jermaine.

"Brother Stokes, we have faith and that is why-"

"We have what?" Jermaine asked his voice full of disgust." My brother had faith and he still got three in his chest because a cop claimed he saw a gun when all he was holding was a cellphone. We had faith the day we watched that pig walk out of court a free man while my brother was under six feet of dirt. My mother had faith in you when you told her to drop the lawsuit and forgive. I lost my faith the day I watched her die in her bed in pain because we couldn't afford the cancer treatment she needed. I don't have faith in you or the white version of God you serve. I believe in the God that sent us Bryson Kane. I believe in the God that gave a black man the strength to stand up for his people and say we are not going to take it anymore. So, I hope you like it hot Pastor because you are the false prophet here. He has never once claimed to speak for God, he speaks for us. The people who have been beaten down by every race of every nation for thousands of years. While people like you are shouting that God will save us, he and those with him are feeding the hungry, healing the sick, and giving shelter to the homeless. All things the church is supposed to be doing but instead you are here tearing down the work of a man who is willing to give everything for his people to have better lives. You are a fucking joke. I stand with the Tide and I will go and do my God's work where it matters while you do your best to keep our people in chains, house nigga."

With that, he puts the hood on and walks down the center aisle and out of the church. The church sits in utter silence for a full minute after he was gone before the Pastor speaks again.

"That my brothers and sisters is a prime example of following a false prophet." he says into the mic, but Victoria could tell he was shaken. "Let us take a moment to bow our heads and pray that Brother Stokes finds his way back to Christ before it is too late."

Everyone stood but not everyone bowed their heads. Many pushed their way passed those who did and proceeded to follow Jermaine out the door. Some had their arms grabbed as family and friends tried to stop them, they just pulled away from them as kept moving. The church watched in stunned silence as over half its number walked out. Victoria never did hear what her dad said after that since she and other members of the choir left the stand and slipped out the back door. She was confused but she felt something guiding her feet as she left the church and went to do God's work where it mattered. She did not agree with the violence, but she would do what she could to help her fellow man. She knew her father would never look at her the same again, but she prayed God would smile down on her and see that her intentions were pure. Jermaine was right it was time they cast off their chains and stood together. Bryson Kane and his Black Wolves had put everything on the line for them and without asking anything of them except that they remember who they were and from where they came. So, if there was ever a time to stand as one it was now.

President Deckland is seething in the Pentagon War Room as the idiots around him are telling him that not only has his military been hamstrung but all of the modern defensive and offensive technology that has made them the world's most powerful nation is being rendered useless in the face of the Tide. A week into this conflict and they were being treated like children getting their toys taken away. No matter what they tried Bryson Kane had an answer to it. They had lost jets, drones, soldiers and vehicles to this man no one could do a damn thing about it. They had lost New York City, the greatest city in the world is now in the hands of terrorists. Gerald had watched as one by one each bureau was taken over.

The Black Wolves unleashed yet another surprise in New York not only was it thousands of them but somehow and of course no one could fucking tell him how they had hidden an army of battle-ready robots all over the city. At first, it was thought they had just highjacked robots that tens of thousands of New Yorkers had bought but these were not robot maids, nurses, or even Lawbots. These were full military custom Battlebots. Neither the Federal Police nor the military would have had a chance even if their weapons still worked which they did not. It was like watching a scene from a sci-fi movie. The scene was repeated all over the world as city by city fell to the Tide. It was just another slap in the face from that egomaniac Kane since he had not shown this kind of power when he took over Georgia. This was him proving yet again that he could end this whenever her wanted but he would rather watch them suffer.

Gerald looked around at the white faces looking back at him. He had honestly never liked black people no matter what status they held on life. This situation had given him a reason to enact Sanction 45 and therefore gave him the powers once held by kings of old Europe. He had already disbanded congress and he had every black member of the Department of Defense in any position of power arrested and taken in for questioning. He had wanted to have every black person who worked within the government period arrested but he was talked down. Instead, he got rid of the one's closest to him. Bryson Kane was receiving help and information from somewhere. He even had the blacks on his Secret Service detail replaced and rotated to other postings where they would not be privy to anything of importance. The War Room computers were manned by white personal all of whom had been vetted and the computers themselves had been taken apart and wiped by white members of DARPA. All their devices had been taken and replaced with new ones that had been scrubbed clean of anything made by Black Tide and any of the dozens of companies connected to it. This room was now one of the most secure in the country if not the world and still President Gerald did not feel safe. He felt trapped like a rat, him once the most powerful man in the world was now cowering in a hole below the Pentagon because the people, he trusted to handle this, were fucking useless.

"So, what you are telling me is that none of you have any fucking idea what to do?" says Gerald his voice low and full of venom. "That the entire Department of Defense has no fucking idea what the fuck to do about one uppity nigger and the fools who follow him?"

Gerald had always liked the way the word nigger tasted coming out of his mouth. Now, it tasted like bile, not because he felt shame for saying it but because it no longer represented an inferior race. How could a race that bred a man like Bryson Kane be inferior to anyone?

"Sir, as my report said the Tide is made of far more than black people." said Felix McCoy the head of the Federal Investigation Division formally known as the Federal Bureau of Investigation before the creation of the Federal Police. "They have members of every race in their ranks. They don't even just fight for black people that is just the race they see as the most oppressed, but they fight for all oppressed people."

The glare Gerald gave him could have melted steel, "I did not ask you for an essay on their cause and I don't care who is among them." Gerald growls. "I want to know how we kill them and take our country back."

"Well sir I feel that understanding them is the first step in doing that." persist Felix." We have tried strong-arm tactics. They failed because Bryson

Kane had already cut off our arms. He poisoned the water, and we have to figure out how. All of this is not something he could do alone. Not in a hundred years and not without us finding out about it. We need to understand how this happened so we can stop it."

Gerald understood what the man was saying, and, on some level, he knew he was right but at the same time, he was well on his way to being the President that lost the county.

"You work on that but in the meantime, I want ideas that end with Bryson Kane dead. If we kill the leader the rest will fall."

"I believe I have a suggestion Mr. President." General Martin Banks Commandant of the Marine Corp says. "A few days ago, I ordered that three teams of a special division of the Marine Corp called Hunter infiltrate Georgia on foot. They are all armed with weapons that don't use chips and communication devices that do not use modern networks. I have just gotten confirmation that one of these teams has made it into Atlanta. They are also carrying neutron bombs sir."

The room goes silent at the mention of the weapon of mass destruction. The weapons had been outlawed worldwide, but that did not apply to America. Research and development had proceeded in secret for decades. Gerald knows that many in the room did not have to stomach to go this far, but he did.

He stands up and gestures to General Banks, "Finally, someone with a fucking brain in their skull." he yells looking at the others who all stare like idiots. "General, I could kiss you right now. However, you are communicating with them. Tell them that they have full authority to do whatever they have to in order to kill Bryson Kane even if they have to bring that whole damn city down to do it."

Captain Rosemary Kirk stands at the window of the abandoned fifth-floor apartment in downtown Atlanta. She was looking out at Black Tide Tower which was about two miles to the east. Behind her the five members of team Hunter 9 were resting and checking equipment. Down below the streets of downtown were not teeming with life like they once were but there was still far more activity than they expected. The powers that be could not get any drones in to get their own intel and they had refused to acknowledge that the citizens of the city were not suffering. But the Marines had seen it with their own eyes as they came in, the people were being given food, water and shelter. The only thing that really changed was instead of police the streets were being patrolled by Black Wolves and reprogrammed Lawbots.

"Captain I got a link." says her communication specialist Rudolph Colon. "We only have a five-minute safe window."

She walked over to where the man was sitting in front of outdated ruggedized laptop with a satellite phone that was just as outdated, jacked into the side. The phone was able to connect to a ghost satellite that belonged to the United States military. It was one of the last ones in orbit and was recently pulled back into service. They checked and double-checked to make sure that it was not compromised by the Tide. It now functioned as their only secure method of communication in the field.

"Hunter 9-1 to Stronghold." Rosemary says into the phone. "We have reached objective and are awaiting orders."

"Hunter 9-1 this is Stronghold." female voice replies. "Statues report, what are you seeing?"

"The city is under guard as expected." her voice is calm and controlled . "The citizens are being treated fairly and cared for. We have eyes on the building believed to be the targets headquarters. City is heavily defended but the new cloaking tech worked well we got in without having to engage enemy forces. Has the primary mission changed?"

There is a silence on the line and then a new voice comes over the line.

"Hunter 9-1 this is Marine Alpha, do you read?" says General Martin Banks.

Rosemary reflexively snaps to attention at the sound of his voice.

"Yes, sir I read you." she ignores the looks her team is giving her.

"Your mission is a go; you are ordered to do whatever is necessary to take out the target, including Payload detonation."

"Yes, sir."

"Good luck and Godspeed Hunters, your country is grateful for your service."

The line goes dead and Rosemary gives the phone back to Rudolph. She looks at the black case in the corner that is carrying a portable neutron bomb powerful enough to wipe out five miles of Atlanta.

She looks around at her team, "We are a go, and we are cleared to use whatever means necessary to kill Bryson Kane." she looks at the case again. "Even if we have to use our last resort."

Zephrah dodged Vin's punches as the bigger man came at her hard. She took one step to the side as he aimed a straight punch at her face. She twisted her hips and drove a knee into his gut doubling him over after bringing him down to her level she drove an elbow into the back of the big man's neck. He fell onto the mat out cold joining the other four men she had already put on their asses. All five of the men were Elite Black Wolves like her. Bryson kept no personal guards but when he wanted something handled, he always turned to his Elites. He had handpicked and trained them all personally. The sub-leaders of the Tide are picked from this group. Zephrah was his best student and his favorite, of course. The entire time she had been there the only person to ever beat her in anything was Bryson himself. No matter how hard she tried she could never beat him and that is what drove her to try harder. She is the official leader of the Elites and it was her job to remain the best in order to see that Bryson's dream was fulfilled.

"Damn, Tiny Terror you are in a mood today." says Craig Ganz her second in command. "You and the boss get into it again."

He tosses her a bottle of water and a towel as she steps off the mat. Zephrah has her long golden dreads tied back in a ponytail and was dressed in a tank top and tights. They are on the training floor of the tower which had been fully given over to its true purpose as the headquarters of the Tide. Each floor had been turned into a different area of operations.

"No, but his patience with these people is starting to rub me the wrong way." she says as she sits on a padded bench. "He could have literally ended this in days and instead he is dragging this out trying to give these idiots a chance to accept his ideas peacefully. I understand that he wants to spare lives, but this world is not going to accept the change it has to be forced on them."

This was a point that many generations of the Elites had argued with Bryson on. It was also one that he had kept in check for generations. The reason he made the Elite was to have individuals who he could share his ideas with at their purest. There were literally thousands of them at any given time and right now they were spread around the world waiting to do his will. Many among the Black Wolves believed that he had given them some special gift like some of his immortality or superpowers but in truth, he had just shared his stories and dreams with them. That was something that all of them felt honored by. He revealed to her that he always chose his Elite based on the fact that he could feel a special connection with them. Which explains why the majority of his Elite were Blooded. Those of them who were given his blood as children were connected to him for their entire life. Some would say this was brainwashing but they all knew differently. If anything, it affected him more than it did them, he could feel it every time one of them died and since they were all like his children it was like losing a child every time. That was why he acted with such patience because to him he was not fielding simple soldiers he was sending his own children into battle. Even those that were too old to be Blooded were like children to him. In truth, he had been a warrior many times over, so he had no mercy for those he saw as his enemies. But as a warrior, he knew that no matter how careful you were death is a part of war. So far, his patience had paid off and they had the world by the throat still it had not been bloodless. Their technology was superior, but hundreds had been lost in combat around the world, a small price to pay for all they had accomplished but still a price. Still knowing all that she did, it pissed her off that he took this slow dragged out approach.

"He is a good man and a good father Zeph." Craig says as he watches the others pull themselves up off the mat. "You have to remember that he has had to show patience for longer than any of us can imagine. He has lived and watched and waited for this moment. The world is his home and even though the black race is his priority he has lived among all races. He doesn't even see Africa as his home anymore, the world is his home and it's people are his people. He is so much more than a man and yet he still carries himself like one. The most humble and compassionate one I believe to have ever lived. So, let him wage this war as he sees fit. He has earned that."

This side of Craig always surprised her, but she was always grateful for it. He was right of course, and her anger disappeared again just as it always did. She was not even truly angry with Bryson; she had no right to be. She was angry because they lived in a world where a man like him could come and talk all the sense and still the world would do anything to keep things the way they were. She shouldn't be surprised this world killed anyone who tried to change it. Well, Bryson could not die as he was fully prepared to cut the cancer out if need be, but he was also willing to treat the sickness with kindness and wisdom. That balance was what made him different from anyone that came before him.

"When did you get so damn wise old man?" she asked and threw her towel on his face.

"Oh, you know me, I have my moments when the wisdom of Kane strikes me." he says from under the towel.

Zephrah laughs and her phone buzzes. She pulls it out and checks the message. She lets out a low growl and Craig peeks from under the towel.

"Action?" asked Craig.

Zephrah stands and walks toward the elevators.

"Get a team ready." she says over her shoulder. "It would seem we have some unwanted guests. They have sent kill teams after Bryson."

Craig's attitude changes instantly as he starts yelling orders. While Bryson is immortal, he is still their leader and they loved him like a father. Anyone foolish enough to come after him would face their wrath.

Tyanna is standing in front of the mirror looking at herself. She is wearing a yellow dress with matching heels. After an hour in her in-home salon, her braids are freshly done and tipped with yellow highlights and she has yellow nails on her hands and feet. She knows she is beautiful, but she still feels nervous after all she wasn't just going to an ordinary dinner.

Her day had been a whirlwind from start to finish. When she went into the news station and gave her video to Perry, she had watched with him just as enraptured by Bryson's speech as the first time she heard it. When it was over and she relays Bryan's request, he personally walked the video over to the morning production crew. It had been aired across the entire network and had even been picked up by broadcast partners around the world. Unfortunately, only those living in U.S cities occupied by the Tide were able to see it since the President had ordered that every news station broadcast government-approved propaganda only. To be sure this order was followed they had taken over every broadcast node outside of the occupied areas. They had ever blocked public access to the internet leaving most of the nation blind to what was truly going on. Tyanna had never thought she would see the day America sank so low, but here they were.

Her phone rang and she saw Bryson's name appear. She picks it up and hits the answer button.

"Hello, there Mr. Overlord." Tyanna says jokingly.

"Overlord." Bryson says as if he were tasting the word. "Overlord Kane does have a nice ring to it. I was shying towards Emperor, but I think I like that better."

Tyanna laughed as she put a few things in her handbag.

"Emperor huh, I thought of you more as a king or chieftain personally." she picks up a slim camera and considers it before putting it to the side.

"All very tempting, we can talk about it when you get here. I was going to come to you, but my people tell me there is a security issue. So, I have been ordered to stay inside tonight. I will be sending a car to come and pick you up. I figured I would just make you dinner instead. Would that be okay with you?"

Tyanna's heart leaped as her excitement and fear rose in equal measure. Excited to be invited to his home but afraid of whatever could make his people keep him there.

"I would love to see your home and I have to say I am even more interested in tasting your cooking."

"I promise it will be edible, see you soon."

The line disconnects and a few minutes later there is a knock on her door. She grabs her bag and heads downstairs.

CHAPTER 6

I am standing in my kitchen listening to music and drinking water while the food cooks when I hear the elevator ding behind me. I know it is Zephrah and I speak without looking around.

"So, you find whoever it is you are looking for?" I asked as I down the rest of my water.

She had told me about the security threat but refused to go into detail. Telling me that she and the other Elites had it handled, and I should just enjoy my night. It was annoying but I knew it was no use arguing with her. She is my right hand and of all the people I keep around me I trust her above anyone else. In family terms, she is my favorite child, and she knows it.

"We are running them down." Zephrah says. "I'll tell you about it in the morning. You just worry about enjoying tonight."

I turn and see that she is wearing the power armor specially designed for my Elites. It is made of a lightweight but incredibly tough metal designed and patented by my company. The armor fits her like a black glove but allows her a full range of unhindered motion. Her speed and strength are enhanced to an incredible level and it has enough built-in weaponry to conquer a small country. It is a nasty bit of hardware and when used by someone as dangerous as Zephrah it is a weapon of mass destruction.

"I will leave it to you then, try not to have too much fun."

"I am not out there to have fun." she smiles at me. "I am just doing my duty: keeping you and your growing empire safe."

I give her a look and her smile broadens.

"I am not building an empire Zeph, only a world where everyone can be equal and free."

She keeps smiling as she walks over and leans on the counter looking me in the eye.

"I love you with all my heart and I live to make your dream a reality, Old Man" her voice is serious. "But I will tell you again at the end of all of this when the world is changed it will still need government and order. I know you believe that we will step up to govern and keep the order while you fade back into the shadows and that may work for a while. But how long will it be before we are at each other's throats because one of us feels the family needs a new head. We are only human, but you are so much more. You even said it in your interview today, you know that you will have to take the role of leader. So, even if you don't see yourself as an emperor you are building the greatest empire of all time and if you turn your back on it, it will crumble and this world will be cast into the flames of war hotter than any before it. You cannot unleash this kind of power and leave it without a guiding hand that is more than human."

I look into her eyes and I want to tell her she is wrong. But I cannot just like I couldn't the first time she shot down my plan. I had been building towards this for thousands of years. In all that time I have seen more of human nature than any living being. I have witnessed evils beyond explanation. I have watched a man sent down to do nothing but good in this world be executed, because he taught what it, meant to be, a member of his religion instead of allowing it to be used as a tool for the greedy. I watched as silver, gold, oil, and land became worth more than human lives. I hope that the world I am building will be different, but I am not that naïve. That has been stripped from me. Zephrah is not the first to tell me this. I have had to hunt down my own people and put a stop to them in the past as they tried to make my dream a reality themselves. All of the world's greatest evils started with good intentions. I am determined not to let mine lead to the greatest evil of all. So, no matter how hard I deny it, I do know that one day I will have a title. I was joking on the phone with Tyanna about it, but it is no laughing matter. Billions would look to me to fulfill the promises I have made them, and I would have to be here to do that not watching from the shadows as I have done for millennia. While I consider all this Zephrah eats from my fruit salad as she continued to stare into my eyes.

"Get lost." I go to pull my food from the oven.

" Yes, sire." her voice is full of satisfaction.

I flip her off and I hear as she activates her helmet. I turn and see her walking to the huge wall window, and it opens to her nonverbal command. She then simply steps out of it and disappears as she drops. A few seconds later I watch as she floats back up using the armor's built-in flight system. She gives me a wave before turning and taking off. The window closes and about a minute later I hear the chime that signals that someone is requesting to be allowed up in the elevator. I check the screen built into the countertop and see that it is Tyanna waiting at the door to my private elevator in the lobby. I hit the flashing green button beside the video display and watch as the door opens, and she steps in. I put the thoughts of the future to the back of my mind for now and focus on the present. The elevator doors open a little under a minute later and Tyanna steps out. I am not ashamed to say my jaw dropped when I laid eyes on her. No matter how long I live the sight of a beautiful black woman will always make my heart race.

"I was prepared to serve a sneaky reporter, not a queen." I said with a smile

Tyanna dropped her head to hide her embarrassed blush, "I am not sneaky thank you very much." She still hides her face. "And thank you, I haven't dressed up like this in a while."

I walk over to her and with a finger under her chin I gently tip her head up so that our eyes meet. I am tempted to kiss her but restrain myself and instead, I brush my thumb lightly over her cheek.

"You are absolutely beautiful." I see her eyes light up.

There is nothing I love more than seeing a black woman understand that she is appreciated. It is something so simple and yet so rare in this day and age. I lead her by her hand to the dinner table and pull out her seat for her. The only ones there are me, her, and my one robot Max. The music stops playing through the speakers and Max steps out with a violin which he starts playing softly.

"Oh my God that is so beautiful." she looks at the robot who is dressed in a full tux. "I have never heard one play before."

"Most can't yet, but Max is the first of them." I look over at robot friend. "He was the first-ever created by Black Tide and every advance since has started with him. Music is not as simple to recreate as people think. It takes not only skill, but passion and recreating passion has taken years, but I think we finally nailed it. Would you like some wine?"

"Yes, red if you have it." she is still watching Max.

"I am pretty sure I can scrounge up something." I hit a button on the counter.

The right wall of the kitchen opens up revealing a huge wine rack full of bottles. Tyanna looks over to it and her mouth drops.

"Impressive considering rarely ever drink, right?" I walk over and picking up two bottles." PETRUS POMEROL 2011 or 2010 Domaine Armand Rousseau Pere et Fils Chambertin Clos-de-Beze Grand Cru?"

I hold the bottles out for her to see and I have to hide a chuckle as her eyes go wide.

"Jesus, do you know how expensive both of those are?" she asked.

I look at them and then back to her and shrugged. Honestly, I have no clue how much most of these are worth. I received most of this wine as gifts from people I have done business with or charities over the years. Once you live through a time period where there were few drinking options other than wine or water, the former becomes very unappealing.

"I assume expensive, I really don't drink the stuff I get it and put it on the rack." I say. "I usually just regift it or use it for nights like this. Some of them are good for cooking I will admit."

She points to the second one and I slide the other back and open the one she picked. I pull down one of the crystal wine glasses and placed it in front of her. After I pour the wine, I leave the bottle in easy reach for her.

"Enjoy, the food will be ready in a minute." I move back into the kitchen to finish up.

I feel her eyes on my back as I move, and I know her mind is full of questions.

"I know you have a lot of questions and I don't mind answering." I start plating the food. "Let's keep the camera down till after dinner. I would hate for the world to turn against me because they see what a slob I am at the table."

"I actually didn't bring a single camera." Tyanna says smiling at me as she sips her wine. "This is amazing, I use to be a food and wine critic before I got my break. I guess you never really lose it because I can tell you that you could have easily gotten double what this bottle was worth."

"Well, your enjoyment is worth far more than that to me." I put the food down in front of her. "I am shocked to hear you didn't bring a camera. I thought for sure your editor would want another exclusive."

I put my plate down and take my seat.

"He did but I told him to shove it." she says with a smile. "It is not every day that you get invited to the home of the richest man in the world for dinner. You, Mr. Kane, are a mystery to me and I want to figure you're out. People are usually more open when they are in private than when they are in public."

Her eyes are both intense and playful all at once. This is only my third time meeting this woman in life but my attraction to her is almost painful. She is beautiful and has an intelligence to match it. I spent a good part of the day going over her news stories and every last one was captivating and in-depth. She is a seeker of the truth and in her own way a champion of our race. So, I decided to trust her with the truth. I watch as she takes her first bite of her meal.

"This is amazing!" she practically shouts as she chews.

I let her swallow before I speak.

"Yes, will I have had nearly seven thousand years to perfect the art."

She looks over at me with her next bite hovering inches from her lips. I just smile at her letting my words register as I take a bite of my own food.

"Ok this wine must be more potent than I thought." she says. "Because I could swear, I just heard you say seven thousand."

She picks up her glass and smells it again. I have a hard time not laughing at the look on her face. I have done this quite a few times throughout my long life, so I have seen all the reactions. They still entertain me though.

"No, you heard me right." I say as I sip my apple juice. "I am 6,976 give or take a few years."

She is now looking at me like I am insane. I am pretty sure I can guess what is going to be said or done next, but I love seeing it. She puts down her fork and drops her head smiling. She then wipes her mouth and looks at me.

"I knew it was too good to be true." she shakes her head. "You are handsome, charming, rich, and insane. I knew it was too good to be true. So, how long have you believed you were immortal Mr. Kane?"

She sits back in her chair and downs her wine. The condescension in her voice doesn't make me angry and I can't blame her so instead of trying to convince her with words I decide to just show her. I swallow another mouthful of food and then I pick up a steak knife and stand up. I step away from the table and unbutton my shirt. She watches me confused and a little lustful. I open the shirt completely revealing my chest and abs to her. It is not a secret that I am a good-looking guy and one of my gifts is my body is always at the peak of fitness, so her attention is fully on my chest and abs. So, I stab myself directly in the gut driving the knife in up to the hilt. The pain is incredible but all I let out is a grunt. Tyanna, on the other hand, screams at the top of her lungs. I let go of the knife and hold my hands out to the side. She sits there with her shaking hands over her mouth completely frozen in fear. I let out a breath and the pain is gone as my next gift activates. The knife is slowly pushed out completely on its own until it falls to the floor. Then, Tyanna watches the blood that flooded from the horrible wound flow in reverse back into the hole and the hole itself closes.

"What?" is all she can manage to say as she walks over to me.

She looks up at me and I just give her a nod. She slowly reaches out and touches the spot where seconds earlier I had just rammed a five-inch steak knife into my gut. There was no trace that the wound had ever been there. She looks back up into my smiling face and then down at the knife on the floor, it did not have a drop of blood on it. My gifts had advanced over the millennia to the point that drawing blood had to be done either with a needle or as soon as the wound was inflicted. If not contained every last drop would attempt to return to my body. She bends down and picks up the knife. She checks it attempting to bend the blade to see if it was plastic or some kind of props.

"Stab me yourself if you like." I am completely serious. "No matter where you put the blade the result will be the same."

She looks at me and then she drops the knife. Her face turns from confusion to a mask of rage and the right hook takes me in the jaw before I can even react. I have to say that was a surprise.

"You fucking jerk!" she screams. "Who the fuck just stands up at dinner and stabs themselves like it is a fucking party trick?"

I look at her and see the tears in her eyes. She was angry yes, but also utterly terrified.

"I am a fucking idiot." I think to myself.

"Tyanna, I am sorry." I reach out to her, but she backs away from me.

I have been around every race of woman and their reactions while angry is not universally alike, but they are very similar. So, I drop my hand and back away giving her space to breathe and process. She looks at me for a while and then turns and walks back to the table. She pours herself another glass of wine and downs it. Then she pours another and drinks half of it before turning and glaring at me. I sit on the back of the couch doing my best to look like a whipped puppy. No matter how old I get the tears of a woman will always be my kryptonite especially if I am the cause of them and an angry black woman will always be my greatest fear. Immortal or not an angry black woman will find a way to make you pay, ask me how I know. Max was still playing in the background and it was a full minute before she was composed enough to speak again.

"So, you are really immortal?" her voice still shaky, but I can tell she is forcing herself to be calm. "And you are really nearly seven thousand years old?"

"Yes, it is all true." I look up to meet her eyes. "I apologize for that display. I honestly figured it would be the fastest way to prove I wasn't lying. I have done it before, and I never really got that reaction."

"Yeah, well sorry for not being understanding about watching you stab yourself."

" Sorry."

There is another stretch of silence and she retakes her seat. She picks up her fork and looks over at me.
"Please, come sit down and let's just have dinner." she says. "We can talk after because I feel like I will need my full attention for this story."

I stand and start to button my shirt.

She raises a hand to stop me, "You can leave that unbuttoned, I am enjoying the view." she gives me a teasing smile. "Call it payback for your stunt."

I smile at her impressed by this woman. I had always been attracted to strong women and she is overflowing with strength and confidence. I leave the shirt open as I walk back and take my seat. We start eating again in silence, but it is not uncomfortable. I catch her eying me and I openly admire her back. After about fifteen minutes we are done, and I take her out onto the balcony to serve her dessert. The night view of downtown Atlanta is beautiful, and we eat dessert in the same comfortable silence. I can tell she is formulating a list of questions and I let her decide when she is ready.

"Where do you come from really?" she asked finally breaking the silence. "I know your bio says you were born here in Georgia and then raised in an orphanage. But, obviously, that isn't true. So, where were you really born and what is your real name?"

I look out at the view and remain silent for a while. Many of the buildings that made-up the downtown Atlanta skyline are now being repurposed, but I had the crews leave the lights on simply because I always enjoyed the view. I look at her as I start to tell my story.

" My earliest memory is waking up floating in an underground cave floating in water. When I ventured out into the world for the first time, I found that I was on the continent that would one day be known as Africa. It was a different place then, truly the birthplace of civilization, but it was also the birthplace of issues that would plague the world for millennia. Back then I went by the name Har. It was given to me by the first people I came in contact with. From the very beginning I always had the urge to watch and learn. Never to truly be a part of the world but to move through its shadows and see how it developed. I saw the tribes of Africa as my people and yet I knew I was not one of them not truly. I never aged, I never got tired, I never got sick, not even the animals of the jungles were a match for me. I am faster, stronger and smarter than anyone I have ever met. Also, I was never content with sitting still I always wanted to explore, to see the changes that came as the years passed but still, I kept my distance. There was evil even then, strong tribes enslaved weaker ones or just wiped them out. They spilled blood in the names of gods they claimed to speak too. I watched this and often helped where I could, but something never let me go as far as I could have. I could've taken control, built an army and started all this then but I was always kept from taking things that far and always returned to the shadows where I watched. To this day I can't explain what that something was."

I stop and look at her and see her staring at me as if mesmerized. Seeing that she was not going to interrupt me and was willing to just sit and listen I continued. I told her how I watched as entire civilizations rose and fell. How I saw men and woman worshipped as gods use their power to enslave those who they deemed inferior. Watched and fought in wars that saw cities burned and entire peoples wiped out. How slowly my purpose in life was revealed to me. I told her how I watched as Africa was slowly invaded and how it's people were put in chains by outsiders and how they were so divided that they stood no chance. It was the beginning of a long and painful cycle that would see the mighty and beautiful nation dying a slow and agonizing death all while I was forced to watch. I told her about my first time traveling outside of Africa and seeing the rest of the world and how I truly started to walk the path that would one day bring me to where I am today. I told her of my blood and how I used it to build a network of people that would one day spread across the world and whom I would come to see as my family. I told her of how I loved many only to watch them pass and fade to dust while I had to keep living for the future of my people.

    I said somethings I have never shared with anyone simply because when I spoke to her I felt something I had never felt in my thousands of years of life: I felt totally at peace. I talked and she listened and then she was in my arms. I have loved many women in my life but when I looked into her eyes, I saw something that I had heard about many times: a kindred spirit. When our lips touched for the first time it felt like I was kissing the sun. The heat was so intense it was painful but neither of us pulled away. I picked her up and she wrapped her arms around my neck.

    We broke our kiss, "I need you." my voice was normally strong, but now it is breaking. "I have never needed anyone more than I need you right now."

    When she speaks her voice is as strong as a hurricane and yet as gentle as a breeze. I look into her eyes and I see a guiding light.

    "I think I have always been yours." she caressed my cheek. "If you need to hear me say it then listen closely. I am giving myself to you now and every day after. You have had those willing to walk this path with you only so far. I promise you I will walk it with you until the end."

    I carried her inside and took her to my bed. Not being able to wait a moment longer. I lay her down gently and ease myself down onto her. I use my arms to hold myself up keeping my full weight off of her as we continue to kiss. She runs her hands up and down my arms and over my chest and abs. I move slowly savoring every inch of her as I kiss my way down her body unzipping her dress and sliding it down as I go. I stand up and pull it off over her heels. I smile down at her as I remove my shirt. She lays there in a matching black lace bra and pantie set with her heels still on. I kick off my shoes and undo my belt taking off my pants and boxers all at once. I stand before her in the dim light of the room completely naked and her eyes roam up and down my body and settle on my steel hard cock.

"See something you like?" I ask with a smile.

"Oh, yes I definitely do, and he seems very happy to see me as well." she sits up and placing her hands on my thighs. "Why don't we get better acquainted?"

Before I can say anything, she takes me into her mouth and starts to suck me with passion. All I can do is look up at the ceiling and groan as she works her mouth up and down taking my full length. It is the most amazing thing I have ever felt, and I am not just saying that. It is like everything she did was a new experience for me. I have no idea how else to describe it. I have had sex thousands of times and yet with her, I felt like a virgin again. She kept going until I gently took her head and stopped her pulling myself out of her mouth. She actually looked up at me and pouted.

" Excuse me I wasn't done." her voice is so bratty I have to laugh.

I push her gently but firmly back onto the bed, get on my knees, and slowly remove he panties. I look her in the eyes as I slowly lower my head between her legs. She lets out a moan of pleasure as my mouth finds its target. She is already soaking wet when I start to work her over with my tongue. Her legs are on my shoulders as I eat her slowly. I take my time alternating between licking her clit and exploring her depths. Tyanna squirms and moans like crazy and then she grabs my head and lets out a scream as her first orgasm rips through her. I drink all of her juices and I keep licking her all the way through it.

"Oh God, I have never felt…oh shit." she pushes me away and crawls back in the bed to get away from me. "Pause, pause what the hell? I have never had an orgasm that intense in my life. Fuck, it was incredible. What the hell did you do to me, Bryson?"

She looks at me as I stand up and run my hand over my mouth. My beard is soaked with her juices and I just give her a wolfish grin. She reaches back and undoes her bra, takes it off, and tosses it to me. I take a deep whiff of it before I toss it across the room. I let out a growl from somewhere low in my throat and I see her visibly shiver as I get in the bed and crawl towards her. She lays back on the bed giving herself to me and I gladly accepted. She runs her hands through my hair and over my body as I focus on mapping every inch of her body with my mouth. When I come back up to kiss her lips, she holds my head and looks me in the eye.

"I want you inside of me Bryson." her voice low and full of need.

I give her one more kiss before I sit on my knees. I take her legs and put them on my shoulders as I line my erection up with her dripping tunnel. I look her in the eyes as she nods slowly. I slowly push forward, and she lets out a scream as she grips the sheets, but we never break eye contact as I continue to slide into her. Her body accepts me with ease as if it were made for me specifically to be inside of it. I pushed into her until all nine inches disappeared inside of her. I sat still as she had another orgasm and when it was over, I started to thrust slowly in and out of her.

"Fuck, fuck, fuck!" she screams. "What, the fuck are you doing to me?"

She clenched the sheets and beats the mattress as, yet another orgasm built. To be honest I wanted to know what she was doing to me. This wasn't just sex; we were making love. I am not a teenager who falls in love with every female I take to bed and even if I did go down that road it was always much later. But I had fallen in love with Tyanna Lucus somehow and there was no way for me to deny it as we made love all night as both of our worlds changed forever.

CHAPTER 7

Captain Rosemary Kirk and her squad stand in the alleyway looking at Black Tide Tower. They are all completely invisible thanks to their next-generation stealth tech. The Hunters used to always having the best technology on their missions, but the stealth tech, portable neutron bomb, and a few infiltration gadgets were the only advantages they had now. Their weapons are decades old before the mass production and use of electronic weaponry. They wore outdated exo-suits that have been checked over and scrubbed by the best DARPA had to offer. Like that mattered at all as DARPA had proved to be useless in this fight, without their superior technology they may as well throw their PhD's at the Tide. It was like going into battle naked but they were the elite of the United States Marine Corps and their country needed them so they would do their duty.

"The building is where Bryson Kane is believed to be." Rosemary says looking back at her waiting team only able to see them thanks to her digital combat glasses. "You all know the stakes here, so I don't have to explain them to you. That being said our orders are to set the timer on the bomb for one hour that is how long we have to complete this mission. One way or another the target is going down. Make sure that your weapons are loaded with the right ammo. We are not the biggest dogs on the yard, but we will damn sure be taking this bitch back. Rannier light the fuse."

She looks over at her demolition expert Rannier Caldwell. The big black man has been a Marine for nearly twenty years and has fought America's enemies on every continent. His courage is unshakable and his loyalty unquestionable. He had been covering Rosemary's six for nearly five years now as Hunter 9's second in command and demolitions expert. It was no one she trusted more. So, when he stood up and deactivated his cloak she was confused. When she saw the look of utter disgust on his face her blood ran cold.

"I had faith in you Rosey." Rannier says his voice full of disappointment. "I told them you would never give that order. That you would see this for the insanity that it is, and you would stop this."

Rosemary watches as Rannier raises his fist into the air and all around them figures wearing full black power armor appear out of nowhere. Before Rosemary can give a single order every member of her team except Rannier is disarmed and forced on the ground. Their cloaks are deactivated after the takedowns meaning these people could see them without issue. Rosemary tries to struggle but even with the strength increase of her exo-suit, she was like a baby being held down by a giant.

"Rannier, you fucking traitor I will kill you!" she screams from the ground as she glares up at him. "I will cut your fucking head off!"

Then there was a sharp pain on the right side of her head and all she saw was darkness

Zephrah kicks the screaming redhead Marine captain in the head as she walks by her. She retracts her helmet and faceplate with a blink.

"All that noise is just unnecessary." Zephrah says as she steps in front of Rannier. "Well hello there Rannier, you got something for me."
Rannier salutes her with a fist to his chest knowing exactly who she was even though they had never met. They are both Blooded but that just allowed them to recognize each other. The real reason was the Black Web, not to be confused with the Dark Web which has been used for everything from child porn to human trafficking. The Black Web has been how the Tide have communicated since the Internet was created. It was written into the earliest code of what would one day become the backbone of the modern civilized world. It was how Bryson had truly connected them over the last eight decades.

Rannier holds out the case with the keypad facing her. Zephrah reaches out and types in the code, she should not know, on the nine-digit keypad and the case hisses before opening. The inside of the case is glass covered circuitry with a black ball in the center.

"So, this is what they have sent against us." Zephrah studies the weapon of mass destruction.

" Yes, and as I reported there are two more being carried by Hunter 4 out of South Carolina and Hunter 7 out of Florida." says Rannier. "Have you intercepted them?"

Zephrah smiles at him and closes the case.

"Yes, they did not survive the encounter." She gives him a predatory smile. "You did well Rannier, I will be recommending your elevation to the ranks of the Elites."

She looks around at the captured Marines and then back at Rannier.

"I cannot guarantee their safety." her face is serious as she looks into Rannier's eyes. "I have not told him of the situation, but he will not be happy about this. I honored your request to let them prove they are different and listened to this one give an order that would have ended the lives of thousands to kill one. I suggest you prepare yourself for the worst."

Rannier looks at the red head who lays out cold and then at the others who glare at him in contempt. He looks back at Zephrah before reaching up and ripping the United States flag off the sleeve of his combat fatigues. He tosses it to the side and puts his fist to his chest.

"I rise with the Tide and the will of The Immortal is law." he says without hesitation. "She made the choice I never thought she would make. I was wrong and I thank you for your mercy, but I understand that their fates are out of my hands and yours."

Zephrah nods and turns away from him activating her helmet.

"Escort the prisoners to the Tower since they are so eager to visit."

Gage Robertson had not expected his life to change so drastically. He went from a S.W.A.T Sergeant to a prisoner of war to a civilian in an occupied state. The Tide had rose and took all of New York.

Gage had been held prisoner until the entirety of New York City was under control. A feat that took three days. He had been treated so humanely that it brought tears to his eyes. They treated him for the broken ribs that he had suffered at the hands of the Black Wolves, fed and watered him on a regular basis and gave him a phone to contact his family. When the city was taken, he and the others were released and told to go home.

When Gage had made it back to his home, he found Belinda and there kids all there waiting for him. When they hugged him, he had fought through the pain of his broken ribs to hug them back. He kissed them all as tears ran down his face. Belinda told him how when it all started, she had thought she had lost him and that her last memory of him would be her ignoring him. They had held each other for hours after that surrounded by their children.

As the rest of the week passed the Black Wolves started to reestablish order in New York City and the surrounding areas. They set up shelters and mobile medical centers for the homeless and sick. They opened stores and even sent out trucks to deliver food, water, basic goods and even medicine door to door in some areas. All of this was done totally free of charge and people could literally walk into a store, get what they needed and leave. It was all kept orderly by the hooded Black Wolves and the thousands of robots that now roamed the streets. It was an obvious takeover but unlike any other in history the Wolves and the robots only got violent when absolutely necessary. Otherwise, they solved problems with soft but firm words. It was truly incredible to watch.

They went into the worse neighborhoods in the city and cleaned them out with either direct words or precise violence. Gangs were dismantled, drugs and guns were taking off the street, and only those who chose to be hurt were hurt. They broadcasted all of this live on the news without any fear. It did not matter what race they were dealing with they gave everyone the same opportunity and handled everyone with the same offered hand or the same closed fist depending on the choices they made.

They completely shut down Wall Street and closed all the banks in effect bringing the economy of not only America but the world to a screeching holt. In a week they took over the most important city in the world, then the entire state of New York. All with less death than the Federal Police Force had caused over the last year trying to enforce the law. They were so open and transparent about it that it was scary. It made Gage rethink his entire life as he sat with his family watching it all. Then he sat and watched as the government he had spent the majority of his life serving showed its true colors and Bryson Kane showed what it meant to make him angry.

Adrianna Ballard's life had changed dramatically in only a week. She was no longer working two jobs just to pay her bills, she no longer feared for her children's safety when they went outside, and her mother was now receiving the best medical care available free of charge. When the Tide took over Chicago the change had been instant. They had control of the city and many surrounding areas within two days. After that they changed everything, things that it would take the government years to even decide to do they did it in a week. Shelters, mobile hospitals and food was sent out all over the city free of charge. Black Wolves and robots appeared in every part of the city and they cleared out the gangs within a few days. They were all giving the opportunity to surrender peacefully and if they didn't accept that then things got very violent very quickly. For the first time in all the time she had lived in Eaglewood she felt totally safe and she let her kids go play outside like normal kids. She still went out with them, but it was more to see it all for herself. She had never thought she would be able to watch them play with other kids with no fear of them being harmed. The Black Wolves and robots still patrolled the neighborhood, but they were nice and even helpful.

Auntie had returned to them like nothing ever happened after defending them during the police raid. She repaired the hole in the roof and then went back to her normal duties. Anytime they asked her anything she told them exactly what was happening and what was going to happen. They watched as it all came true. On the fourth day the medical team arrived. They were kind and very professional as they requested to take her mother. She had been hesitant, but Auntie had assured her that it was all for the best. She had allowed it and helped Auntie calm her mama as they took her. They had told her where they were taking her and the incredibly expensive treatments she would be receiving. They kept her for two days before Adrianna and the kids were allowed to visit her at Northwestern Medicine Prentice Women's Hospital. Her mother was in better health and higher spirits than she had been in years. They completely eradicated cancer with technology the hospitals usually only kept for patients who could afford to pay outrageous prices that they did not even take insurance for only cash up front. That had pissed Adrianna off but all that mattered to her was that her mother was healthy again. They wanted to keep her for observation and allowed Adrianna and the kids to stay with her.

They were all together watching the news when Bryson Kane's face took over every station. It was the day he became known to the world as The Immortal and the day he showed the world what he was truly capable of.

Tyanna wakes up in the most comfortable bed she has ever been in and her body feeling better than it ever had. As the sun hits her eyes the memories of the night before flood back into her mind and she smiles like a schoolgirl. She pulls the covers up over her face and even kicks her feet in excitement. It had been a long while since the last time she did it on a first date and she had never had sex that amazing in her life. She looks over and sees that Bryson is not there anymore. She remembered falling asleep in his arms and thinking how perfectly safe she felt. Like nothing in the world could touch her. When she looks over, she sees a yellow silk robe folded in the chair by the wall window and some sandals underneath. She gets up and gets dressed noting that everything fits perfectly.

When she walks out of the bedroom, she finds Bryson in the kitchen having breakfast with a young lady and an older guy who are both wearing black power armor. Bryson looks up and smiles at Tyanna as he walks over to her and gives her a kiss that takes her breath away. When it is over, she stares up at him loving his smile.

"Good morning." Bryson says and his voice seem to resonate down to her very soul.

Tyanna knew that it was not normal but at the same time she loved it.

"Good morning." she says back as she hugs him and lays her head on his chest.

When he puts his arms around her, she once again feels like the safest person alive. He stands there holding her until she finally let's go. She looks around him at the other two who watched them with smiles on their faces. Bryson looks back at them and then introduced them.

"Tyanna Lucus this is Zephrah Rogers and Craig Jones. Zephrah is the commander of my Elites and Craig is her second in command."

"Nice to meet you ma'am." they both say in unison.

"Likewise, and please just call my Ty or Tyanna, I am really not that old." she walks over to shake both of their hands. "It is so nice to meet you both."

Bryson had told her a bit about the way his organization was set up the night before. So, she knows the Elites are directly under him in the hierarchy. Bryson pulls out a chair for her and she takes a seat. She notices the three cases sitting on the floor beside Craig. Bryson puts food and juice in front of her and she thanks him. She eats as she listens to their conversation.

"They have proven how low they are willing to go." Zephrah says to Bryson who continues to eat. "It is time you take the kid gloves off and let us flip all this shit over. We could have the entire United States by the end of September, you know I am not wrong."

"You are not wrong." Bryson says as he looks over to Craig.

"I have to agree, I mean they sent three neutron bombs." Craig says gesturing to the cases at his feet. "These are not precise weapons they would have killed tens of thousands if we had not stopped them."

Tyanna drops her fork and stares at the three cases, "I'm sorry what?"

"They are deactivated, babe" Bryson's voice calms her completely but then the fear is replaced with outrage.

"Who sent these?"

"I'll give you three guesses, but I bet you only need one." Bryson takes a sip of his drink. "But I'd like to ask you a favor if I may."
"
Anything." Tyanna answers without hesitation. " Absolutely anything."

CHAPTER 8

I step out of the elevator onto the rooftop of my building wearing an all-black tailored business suit and my usual shades. Dozens of people were waiting for me including Tyanna, Zephrah and Craig. There were also members of U.N.N, Black Wolves and the prisoners taken last night. This last group was seated in the center of the roof with their hands bound. Five Marines belonging to an organization called Hunter. There were six of them technically, but one had been a Black Wolf named Rannier. He is standing with Zephrah and Craig in front of the five Marines. He still wears his combat fatigues and is looking down at a red head who is glaring up at him. The U.N.N crew is setting up camera and broadcasting equipment. Tyanna is speaking with a plump white guy she had introduced as her editor/producer Perry Smith. I walk over to them and both turn my way. Tyanna is dressed much more conservatively than last night.

"Mr. Kane, I have been informed by our company president that the network is willing to play your broadcast nationwide and even worldwide." Perry says. "But the government has taken over all of the major broadcast nodes outside of the areas your people now control. So, they can control what the people see as they have done for weeks. I am sorry they have effectively cut off the government-controlled United States from the rest of the world allowing only government-approved propaganda."

"Is this America or Nazi Germany?" Tyanna rubs her eyes. "We have even heard of people disappearing and rumors of prison camps."

"Those rumors are true." I say and they both look at me with wide eyes. "There are five in total all built in secret over the last twenty years. Officially they are known as rendition camps or black sites used by groups like the Federal Intelligence Agency and the Federal Drug Agency to house and interrogate high-value targets. At least that is their purpose on paper. In truth, they have been used to keep citizens the government has declared to be dangerous to national security as well. Many of whom are thought to be dead, so their families don't look for them. I have people embedded in all of them as guards and prisoners."

"Unbelievable." Perry has to take a seat on an equipment case.

"It is simply how things have been for years now." I put a hand on his shoulder. "But today that all changes. Relay my thanks to your boss for his willingness to help and tell him that after my broadcast his nodes will once again be free to be used. Now, if you all are ready, I would like to begin in about five minutes.

Perry and Tyanna just stare at me. I give them a smile and kiss Tyanna lightly on the lips before turning away. I walk over to Zephrah, Craig and Rannier. Rannier puts his fist to his chest in salute, a gesture the Wolves had adopted over the generations. Zephrah and Craig did not mimic the gesture being on much more familiar terms with me.

"Good work Rannier and I am sorry that your faith was misplaced." I offer him my hand.

He takes it and gives it a firm shake.

"It is an honor to finally meet you sir and thank you."

"Keep smiling while you can traitor because I swear, I will cut your heart out." says the redhead Marine that I know from the reports as Captain Rosemary Kirk, her green eyes flick to me. "Then I will take your fucking head."

I let out an honest to God laugh at this. I have fought in tens of thousands of battles and thousands of wars. I have been taken prisoner hundreds of times most of those were admittedly on purpose but still I understand her anger and her conviction. Though I have never seen myself as a citizen of any nation I have inhabited, I have felt loyalty and even kinship to many peoples and their causes. She sees me as an enemy to everything she has sworn to protect. In truth, she is not completely wrong. I am an enemy to her country the way that is now and the evil that makes up its heart. But she also has sworn to protect all the people of the United States no matter their race and I am not an enemy of that way of thinking. I am an enemy to those of them who spread hate and prey on those whom they see as weak or inferior to themselves simply because of their skin color, where they were born or what they believed. I stop laughing and remove my shades so that I can look her in the eyes.

"You will have your chance to do that soon captain." I say. "But I would advise you to walk the road of peace and not war when that time comes. Because, if you do not, I will show you no mercy."

My eyes sweep over all of the Marines and then they go back to Rosemary. If looks could kill hers would have stripped my soul from my body. I sigh and put my shades back on and turn to Zephrah.

"Have the nodes been taken?"
"Just got the last confirmation five minutes ago." Zephrah replies.

I chuckle knowing that she is relishing what is coming next, "Then let's show them we can do much more than bare our fangs." I walk back over to where Tyanna is waiting. " I am ready whenever you are Ms. Lucus."

Tyanna looks up at me wearing a scowl.

"What did I say?" I ask.

"After last night you are no longer allowed to address me by any form of my government name." Tyanna says seriously.

" Duly noted, well I am ready when you are babe."

She stands on her tiptoes and I bend down to meet her. She gives me a kiss before turning and walking over to the camera set up. I follow her pretty much like a trained puppy I am not ashamed to admit. If you could see the sway in her hips you would understand, believe me. I stop and stand off to the side as she takes her place in front of the camera. Behind her on a table sit the three neutron bombs open and on full display. They mic Tyanna up and Perry comes over to me.

"I have no idea how you did it, but I just got word that every node is back up and ready to transmit." he says. The excitement in his voice barely contained.

"Well I should warn you ahead of time Perry this may get graphic." I reply

I watch as his excitement turns to concern. He looks over at the bound prisoners and I see the light click in his head. He looks back at me and swallows before speaking.

" Graphic like the Federal Court graphic?"

I give him a simple nod and he looks down at his feet. Then he looks over at the three bombs on the table behind Tyanna. When he looks back at me his face is set with a look of determination.

"Whatever you feel you have to do I will make sure the world sees it in its purest form."

"That is all I ask of you and your group Mr. Smith."

I offer my hand and he shakes it. He moves so that one of his people can put a mic on me. When it is done, I give Tyanna a thumbs up. She nods and looks directly at the camera. The cameraman raises his hand. She counts down from five. When he reaches one the red light on the camera turns green meaning, they are live.

"Good afternoon and welcome to U.N.N my name is Tyanna Lucus and I am here to report some breaking news." Tyanna starts and she steps to the side to allow the camera to get a clear view of the cases on the table. "These are portable neutron bombs or Payloads, each of them has blast radius of five miles in all directions. Everything within that blast radius from flesh to steel will be vaporized in an instant if they are detonated. These devices are highly illegal and any use of them is considered a crime against humanity. Last night these three devices were carried into the state of Georgia by three groups of United States Marines working for a covert operations group known as Hunter. They were on a mission to assassinate Bryson Kane and if they found that they could not complete the objective by normal means they were to detonate these explosives. Thanks to the efforts of the Black Wolves two of these groups were eliminated and one was captured, saving the lives of many thousands in the process. Today their leader Bryson Kane would like to speak to the world and make his intentions clear, Mr. Kane."

"Thanks for the introduction babe." I step up into view of the camera.

Tyanna looks at me shocked and even with her dark skin, I can see that she is blushing. I just flash my usual charming smile before turning and looking into the camera.

"Hello everyone and to those of you outside of the states I now control welcome back." I begin to unbutton the cuffs of my jacket. "For those around the world who may be watching, well I know you are watching since I had my people hack most of the worlds broadcast nodes over this past week, I say to you all, welcome. You all know me as Bryson Kane and if you believe the words of the governments currently in power, I am a terrorist and a mad man. I am not here to contradict this. By the standards of today's world, someone who wants to see everyone in this world be treated equally and prosper is completely insane. Well, that someone is me and if being insane is what it takes then insane is what I will be."

I remove my coat and simply drop it to the ground at my feet before continuing.

"I have been around for a very long time. Longer than many of you would or could ever believe. I have seen this world crumble into the cesspit that it currently is. I have watched empires rise out of blood and cruelty. Slavery was the foundation of all of these mighty nations: Egypt, China, Akkadian, Assyria and the list goes on. This world is built on the blood of the weak and the corruption of the strong. The black race in its many forms has taken the brunt of the cruel cycle but they are not the only ones. Every race has experienced slavery at some point in their history but only the black race remained there. Beaten down in every part of the world until they accepted it as normality. Well I am here to break this world and rebuild it the way it should be. Some of you will agree with me and others will say I have no right. To those in the second category I give you this warning. If you stand in my way, I will show you no mercy. The Tide has become a tidal wave and it will drag you under. To those who follow me this name is known but to the rest of you I would like to introduce myself. I am The Immortal and this world already belongs to me. So now you have a choice will you stand with me or against me."

I roll up the sleeves of my shirt and turn to the five Marine prisoners. They are all pulled to their feet and their cuffs are removed. Then the Black Wolves simply back off, leaving the now free Marines looking around in confusion. I gesture for the camera to be pointed at them as I approach.

"You five chose to follow the orders of "sane" men and brought weapons that would've killed thousands just to stop my insanity." I stop just six feet from them. "So, now you will be the first five I offer this choice to: Will you stand with me or against me?"

It is Captain Kirk who steps up and her eyes still carry the same fire and hate. She looks from me to Rannier and then back to me.

"You are a terrorist and you have just proven how insane you truly are." She says as she moves closer to me. "The Immortal, so what are we supposed to believe that you can't be killed? That what, you have walked this world for thousands of years and you witnessed all of this so-called cruelty and corruption firsthand? Please this is nothing but a joke and the fact that all of these lunatics you have around you believe it just proves how insane all of you are. This country is not yours. The United States was built to be the freest nation on Earth, and we have made it our mission to stop tyrants like you by any means necessary. Yes, we brought those bombs, and every man and woman who carried them was and still is willing to give their lives to stop you. We were willing to sacrifice thousands here in order to stop you from killing millions or billions in the war you have declared on the world. You claim to fight for equality for the black race well all I see is another Hitler. He claimed to fight for the white race and yet it was white men and women who stood up to stop him. It will happen all over again black Americans will stand against you and then what will you do? You will murder them just as easily as if they were white. You are not one of them Bryson Kane you are a rich asshole with more money than brains. You ask if we will stand with or against you? Well, the answer is against you like we stand against every tyrant."

The other four step up to stand beside her. They look strong and proud like all warriors do. With their choice made I simply raise my hand and gesture to two Wolves who roll a black weapons case forward. They open it revealing an assortment of close combat weapons. The Marines look at them and then back to me.

"You have made your choice and spoken your peace," I say with a note of finality in my voice. "That is what I and all those who follow me will offer to all of those who wish to stand against me. Now, I will allow you to pick your weapons and fight for what you believe in. I will be your opponent and if you kill me you will go free. If I kill you well, you will just be dead. No one else will get involved unless you try to attack anyone except me. Make your choices I will wait."

I stand with my hands in my pockets and just watch as the five of them move slowly towards the case. They take about five minutes to converse amongst themselves and pick their weapons. Once they have all turned to face me holding their chosen tools of death, I remove my hands from my pockets and hold them out to my sides. Nothing else needs to be said as I wait for them to attack. The Marines slowly move to surround me like a pack of wolves preparing to take down a bear. The first two Danny Warner and Juan Finch attack me from behind. Both of them have shock sticks and they attack from the left and the right. I move without thought, getting low and dodging to the left. I am faster and more agile than any baseline human. So, when I get out of range of their attacks, I close the distance between myself and Rudolph Colon the big white Marine has no time to register anything but shock.

He is holding a force stick and he only manages to raise it an inch before I grab him by the wrist. I gave a savage twist breaking it making him release the weapon with a scream. I catch the weapon by the handle, spin, and strikes him directly under his chin with it. The force stick doubles the impact force of the one wielding it. My strength like my speed and agility is beyond that of a baseline human so when the stick impacts with Rudolph's head it simply explodes like a ripe melon. Brains, blood, and bone fly directly upwards. He is lifted off his feet and the headless body flies fifty feet through the air and over the side of the rooftop. The shield drones that had been set to standby until now move in to stop the blood that starts to rain down from splashing anyone. The blood sizzles and evaporates on the shields. It is really quite disturbing now that I think about it. I look into the shocked eyes of the remaining four Marines and toss the weapon to the ground. Once again, I stand with my hands out to my side.

Erica Patrick takes one step back and I am on her in a second. She is holding twin blades with yellow laser edges. I grab both of her wrists and force her to stab both blades up under her sternum and into her own heart. Her eyes go wide for a moment and then blank as she dies. I release her and let her body fall to the ground. I turn and look at the remaining three Marines all of whom no longer look like wolves as they realize there is a true predator amongst them. Danny and Juan don't even realize that I am in front of them until I grab both of their shock sticks and drive them up under their chins. Both of their bodies go ridged as over a hundred thousand volts of electricity hits their brain. They are both dead before they hit the ground, but their bodies continue to spasm. I turn around and look at Captain Rosemary Kirk who holds a blue laser edge sword in shaking hands. I start to walk towards her, and she backs away swinging the sword wildly.

"Stay away from me you fucking monster." she screams all the anger and contempt in her voice replaced with panic and fear.

When I am in range she stops swinging and stabs at my chest with the blade. The sword goes through the center of my chest and comes out my back. There are screams of panic around us and Rosemary gives me a triumphant grin. I simply glare down at her, completely unbothered by the sword in my chest . She let's go of the sword and backs away from me. I reach up and grab ahold of the hilt of the sword, my eyes still locked on hers. I slowly pull it from my body as if drawing it from a sheath. She stares at my chest in horror when it is completely out, and I feel the horrific wound knit itself back together. I look up to see that the cameraman had changed positions so that he now had a perfect angle. Meaning the world had watched me completely heal from a wound that should have killed me instantly. Rosemary slowly fell to her knees her mouth working silently. When she senses me standing over her, she looks up at me.

"Please, have mercy I have a family." she pleads weakly all her fight gone.

"Then I hope they make better choices than you did." I raise the sword. "May your soul travel swiftly to its resting place."

Before she can speak again, I put the full length of the sword into her throat. It comes out the back of her neck severing her brainstem and sticks into the ground holding her pinned there on her knees. The death is instant but the visual would be burned into the minds of all of those who watched it. I released the hilt of the sword turning off the laser edge as I did. Then I looked around me at all the faces. There was shock, horror, and disbelief there. Some were visibly sick and even passed out. My eyes landing on Tyanna and she just stared back at me with a look of comprehension on her face. She finally understood that I was someone to be feared. Only time would tell how this moment would affect our relationship, I would give her space and let her process it. I had just shown the world what I am and what I can do. I look directly into the camera once again and this time I speak not as Bryson Kane but as The Immortal.

"The choice is yours but know that if you stand against me then you will share the same fate. I am The Immortal, and I am here to take this world. Know that from now on my Black Wolves will be fighting under a Black Flag. The time for talk is over you will either follow us or you will be crushed by the Tide, the choice is yours. To you President Gerald Deckland, I warned you and now I do want your head. I will be coming to claim it very soon. First, you will watch as America is taken from you and the lie of freedom for all becomes a reality. To my Wolves in every American held territory the time for waiting and reacting is over. Take it all!"

PART TWO

CHAPTER 9

President Gerald Deckland watched Bryson Kane's broadcast with a building sense of dread. He watched as he dubbed himself The Immortal and then proceeded to give some self-righteous speech about how the world has mistreated black people. The fact that he was even watching this made him want to rage. He had received reports of the broadcast nodes he had ordered to be secured and co-opted for approved government broadcast only, had all been taken literally overnight. As the broadcast went on the rage turned to dread and then rose to pure unadulterated fear as he watched The Immortal execute the four Marines with brutal ease. He watched as Captain Kirk had ran him through with a sword. He and the Joint Chiefs had stood up and cheered. It lasted only seconds as they then watched The Immortal slowly pull the blade from his chest leaving a hole they could see through even on the screen. Gerald fell back into his chair as he watched the hole disappear as if it had never been there.

"It was impossible."

"It had to be a trick."

"This is madness."

The President watched The Immortal drive the sword through Captain Kirk's neck pinning her in place. Then the monster disguised as a man looked directly into the camera and directly at Gerald. When he spoke, the words stabbed into the President like cold spike.

"The choice is yours but know that if you stand against me then you will share the same fate. I am The Immortal, and I am here to take this world. The time for talk is over you will either follow us or you will be crushed by the Tide, the choice is yours. To you President Gerald Deckland, I warned you and now I do want your head. I will be coming to claim it very soon. First, you will watch as America is taken from you and the lie of freedom for all becomes a reality. To my Wolves in every American held territory the time for waiting and reacting is over. Take it all!"

Gerald stands up ignoring everyone around him and walks over to his Secret Service Director Zachary Richards.

"Get me to Area 51 right now." Gerald says quietly.

"Yes, sir." Zachary says as he gets on his comm and starts issuing orders.

Gerald turns back to the room and sees everyone watching him. He looks around at all of them and then without a word he simply turns around and leaves. The Secret Service detail flanks him as he enters the elevator. The doors close on the stunned faces of the Joint Chiefs.

Jace Cross is a former Army Ranger now working as a guard for Black Site Helo located within the town of Mentone, Alabama atop of Lookout Mountain. The entire town had been bought by the government in 2027 turned into a prison for those the government deemed dangers to national security. It is also campus for those who guard them along with their families if they have them. This prison holds terrorist, assassins, weapons engineers and other threats to not only America but the world. It also holds several people who have done nothing more than spoken up against the American government. This has been going on for decades and has only gotten worse as the years passed.

Jace is sitting in the locker room getting ready to start his shift when Bryson Kane's broadcast began. All around him his fellow guards stopped what they were doing to watch it. Jace having a feeling what was about to happen started removing the uniform he had gotten halfway on and tossed it to the floor. He stood in only his boxers as he opened the black backpack hanging in his locker. From inside he pulls out five pads about the size of playing cards and just as thin. He discreetly placed the five pads on his body the black standing out against his white skin. But anyone looking would most likely think they are something to help his muscles since he is well known gym rat. But almost every eye was looked on the television and those that weren't were busy making their own preparations. Jace pulls a black cellphone from the backpack and puts his hand over the thumb pad . He feels a slight burn as the DNA scanner takes some skin cells and uses them to verify his identity. The phone opens to blank black screen as Jace waits. He hears The Immortal speaking but only the last words truly registered.

" To my Wolves in every American held territory, the time for waiting and reacting is over. Take it all!"

Seconds after he spoke those words a one-word message came across the screen of the phone.

"Attack."

Jace pressed the thumb pad of the phone and the five pads on his body immediately expanded until he was fully clothed in the black hoodie, camo pants, boots, facemask and gloves that is the uniform of the Black Wolves. He closes his locker with a bang and gets the attention of the other guards around him. With his mask on his vision is clear as day despite the glowing red lenses that signaled, he was in combat mode. The threat detection system marked everything with one of five numeral classifications depending on how much danger they posed him. Nothing in his immediate line of site registered above a two. He could feel the presence of three other Blooded in the room with him. He had no doubt they were all ready for what was about to happen as well.

He looks into the eyes of the guard nearest him. A tall, buff Hispanic man named Marcos Villa. Jace knew the man well and really did not like him. He had spent time working undercover Mexico for the Federal Drug Unit and his years of living amongst the cartels had left him broken and cruel. He took pleasure in torturing the prisoners for both amusement and to gain information as a member of the prison's Interrogation Unit. Jace had been responsible for carrying what was left of his victims to the infirmary. Yes, many of the people here were evil bastards who were responsible for true acts of horror. But Marcos enjoyed torturing the people he knew were put there simply because they spoke out and someone in the government didn't like it. Jace was Blooded and so the Immortal Faith was printed on his DNA. He believed that even the worst of people in the world deserved a swift death and that the strong should always protect the weak. Being embedded here had forced him to watch and do nothing as the weak were made into playthings for evil men and women and death was anything but swift.

So, when Marcos took a step back and his hand went down towards his gun. Jace felt fully justified when he blink clicked his power glove up to maximum and drove it into Marcos' chest. He felt bone break as the big man literally flew back and hit the wall so hard his body burst covering the white wall in red blood.

"Are you with us or against us?" Jace asked as an afterthought. "Oh, I was supposed to ask that before I killed him, my bad."

After that all hell broke loose in Black Site Helo as the Wolves went on a rampage.

Staff Sergeant Ina Tanner catches the fire ax in one hand and looks up at the big soldier who had swung it at her. The man attempted to pull the ax away from her and normally it would have been no problem. He was 6'3 and easily 300 and she was 5'5 and just barely 170 pounds. The difference is she is wearing the power armor of an Elite Black Wolf. So, when she yanked the man towards her, he came like he weighed nothing. She grabbed him by his belt and lifted him bodily over her head. She then pile drives him directly on the top of his head. The big man's body twitched and spasmed, but Ina's display told her he was dead.

The poor bastard had tried to surprise her by popping out from around a corner. She turns the corner now and sees five other soldiers there all with guns aimed at her. One was laying on his belly behind an outdated M249 Light Machine Gun. He has two others kneeling beside him and two standing behind them all holding M16 Assault Rifles. She had been here when they pulled the outdated guns out of mothballs and reissued them once the fact that all of their modern weapons were useless against the Black Wolves became an undisputed fact.

"Those will fire but they will not stop me." Ina says her voice amplified through her helmet speakers. "This is your one chance to drop them and surrender. If you do no harm will come to you, I only want Colonel Davis. The base has already fallen there is no need for you to die here."

It was all true her people had taken Joint Base Lewis–McChord already and were now cleaning up the last pockets of resistance. All that was left was her taking down the Command Center and killing or capturing Colonel Clay Davis. The man could've stopped all this when the attack began just by surrendering and ordering his people to stand down. The Black Wolves' attack had come from within and without. It was a dagger to the heart from the start but the agent in the command center had failed because Colonel Davis had gotten on the command channel shouting orders. If he hadn't many of the soldiers would have just surrendered. The Immortal had turned them loose meaning they only offered mercy once. After that pain or death was the only option they gave their enemies. The five soldiers before her were all trained Army Rangers and possibly even spec ops so she knew what was about to happen and it saddened her.

"Fire!" yells the Ranger behind the M249.

They all open fire, and the noise would have been deafening if her helmet didn't muffle the worst of it. The five had made their choice and Ina turned from diplomat to executioner. Activated her armors flight system and let the red laser claws on the tips of each of her fingers activate. She floated up a foot off the floor and then shot forward. The bullets impacted her armor's energy shield like rain on an umbrella and had no effect. Even without the shields, she knew the bullets would not have pierced the armor. Then she was on them her claws flashing. The gunfire was replaced with short screams of pain and then silence. Ina steps over the bodies and walks to the steel door of the Command Center.

The keypad is red meaning the door has been sealed. She puts her hand up to it and lets her armor system hack it. It takes about three seconds and the pad turns green. The door slides open and Ina is met by another hail of gunfire. She just stands there letting her shield do its job as she scans the room. The gunfire is coming from ten separate shooters all of them in cover behind computer stations and all using outdated weapons. She locates Colonel Davis firing on her from the raised command platform. She ignored the others as she flew up to where he was. The Colonel backs away in fear but keeps firing until Ina slaps the gun from his hands and puts an armored hand around his throat. The gunfire abruptly stops as his subordinates realize; they can't fire at her without hitting their leader. The big black man hits Ina's armored arm with hammer-like blows that do absolutely nothing. He stops when she tightens her grip.

"You will get on the comm give the order for all your people to stand down." Ina says firmly as she forces the man to his knees. "This base belongs to The Immortal now. It is no need for more good men and women to die for no reason."

"They are not dying for no reason." Colonel Davis wheezes as he glares up at her. "They fight for their country and to stop a tyrant."

"Tyrant?" Ina is in disbelief. "He is fighting mainly for the people of our race. Don't you see that? Don't you care about our people?"

"He doesn't speak for my people!" he yells as loud as her grip would allow. "He is fighting for lazy niggas who blame everything on racism or want everything handed to them! I am a proud black man who worked my way up out of the gutter! I don't need some psychopath speaking for me!"

Ina heard his words and she felt tears sting her eyes. Then she hardened her heart and activated the claws on her free hand.

"Then we don't need you."

She drives her clawed hand into his chest piercing his heart and killing him instantly. Blood spews from his mouth and splashes her armor. She looks him in the eye until the life fades from them and then lets him go leaving him on his knees with his head down. She looks around the Command Center and sees that hooded Black Wolves had come in and secured everyone else there. She spots the body of Kyle Paul slumped against a workstation a bullet in his head. It looked like they got him before his gear could fully activate. She closed her eyes and mourned him for a few moments before opening them. She blinks and opens a connection to the Black Web Command Net. She marked the base as captured and reported the death of Colonel Clay Davis. When she was done, she opened her comm and started issuing fresh orders as she stood on the command platform. She watches out the window of the Command Center as the American flag is lowered, and the Black Flag is raised. She knows that all over the country the same scene would be playing out over and over as America was ripped apart by the Black Wolves and rebuilt in the name of The Immortal and under the Black Flag of The Tide.

Green Streets Blood shot caller Jekeil "Hyde" Starks puts his gun to the head of the last Triad and pulls the trigger. The man's head snaps back, and his body falls backward joining the rest of the dead Asians on the floor of the stash house. His goons are moving around stuffing drugs and money into duffle bags. This was the third drug den they hit that night and the nineth one in total since the Black Wolves had started their attack on Los Angeles three days before. They were dismantling the Federal Police after they shot multiple Mexicans during an immigration raid. Jekeil hadn't believed it was possible to take the Federal Police on in a straight fight until he had seen it with his own eyes. After Bryson Kane's broadcast earlier that day the takeover not only increased in speed it spread like wildfire. He and the Green Street Blood shot callers had seen their opportunity to settle some scores. Today they were settling up with Eight Dragon Triad, who had been moving in on their territory for months.

"Hurry this shit up, we are on the clock." Jekeil yells

He grabs a full duffle and heads down the stairs to the first floor of the stash house. He finds more G.S Bloods down there waiting for him with guns aimed at the twelve naked Asian women kneeling on the floor with their hands duct taped behind their backs. They were packaging the drugs and counting the money when the Bloods kicked in the front door five minutes earlier. In the corner lay the three Eight Dragon members they had put down on entry.

"Get those bitches in the bathroom and load up."

The Bloods got all the women on their feet and moved them all into the small bathroom in the back of the house. Jekeil heads out the front door into the South LA hood and heads toward the waiting van. A Blood goes to open the side door for him, but he is thrown through the air as something falls from the sky and hits the top of the van. The sound and force of it is like a bomb going off. Jekeil is thrown backwards and lands hard on the front porch of the drug den. Pain shoots through his body, his ears are ringing, and his vision is going in and out. He rolls slowly to his side and struggles to catch his breath. He feels hands grabbing him and pulling him backward. When his ears finally stop ringing and his vision steadies, he realizes he is back inside the house. All around him his goons are panicking, and he doesn't under why. That is until the front door that two of them are holding closed explodes in throwing both grown men like rag dolls. Jekeil is still on the floor covering his eyes to protect them against the flying wood. When he lowers his hand, his heart drops out his ass as he sees a pair of red eyes looking down at him.

"Judging by your heart rate I am guessing that you understand just how fucked you truly are." says the mechanical female voice of the Elite. "We can do this peacefully or you can be stupid, your choice."

One of the Bloods comes out of the bathroom holding one of the naked women at gun point, "Move and she is dead, back the fuck off now."

The Elite walks forward and Jekeil uses his hands to pull himself across the floor out of her way. He tries to fight down the panic rising in his chest. He had watched the U.N.N reports since they started broadcasting again. He knows about the Immortal and those who serve him. He had watched footage of what these people were capable of and he knew they were all in deep shit.

"Oh, look I moved."

Even in the armor the Elite is still the shortest person in the room and nearly every gun is trained on her. But there is no fear in her voice and her stance reminds Jekeil of a waiting predator. There is no doubt that she is the one in charge here. The goon holding the woman backs up dragging the woman with him. He backs away from the Elite until his back hits a window. He takes the gun from the woman's head and aims at the Elite instead.

"Stay back damn it or I-"

He never finishes the threat as the window breaks behind him. A black armed hand grabs the arm holding the gun and squeezes it until it breaks. The man screams and lets go of the gun and the woman. Then he is yanked out of the window and the screaming suddenly stops.

"Now, just to be clear your weapons will not fire and unless you want to end up like your friend you will drop them." the threat in her voice is clear. "I have killed enough people over the last few days and I really do not want more blood on my claws."

Jekeil is now sitting against the wall and her glowing red lenses fall on him again. After a few seconds under her gaze he slowly starts to move again. He gets onto his knees and puts his hands behind his head. His guys all look at him in disbelief. He doesn't give a fuck about any of them at this point, he is saving his own neck. After about ten seconds they start to put their weapons down and drop to their knees one by one. Jekeil is still staring up into the red lenses when the Elites helmet and faceplate retract revealing the face of a young Asian female. Jekeil's fear doubles and suddenly he's not so sure surrender is his best option. He was being taken prisoner by a chink after he had killed a house full of chinks. He feels his backup piece in the holster at the small of his back. Before he can make a move, the Asian Elite speaks.

"Seriously, do you believe you are faster than me, Jekeil?"

Jekeil loses his nerve once again and she just smirks at him. A second Elite enters through the broken window and all thoughts of resistance disappear from the minds of every banger in the room. Five minutes after the attack a group of hooded Black Wolves arrive and take them all into custody. Los Angeles had been taken and the rest of California isn't far behind. The Wolves have turned their attention to reform and clean up, meaning that the gangs were no longer running under the radar.

General Timothy Sparks has served his country for forty years since he was eighteen years old. He fought in every major conflict over the last four decades before he was appointed General of the Army by President Deckland. In all that time he had never seen anything like what he had witnessed today. He and the other Joint Chiefs had watched the President of the United States effectively abandon the country and then in eight hours they saw nearly every Army, Navy, Air Force, and National Guard base fall to the Tide. It did not matter what orders they gave the Tide could not be stopped. They were everywhere and seemed to control everything. After they captured all the major military targets, they turned their attention to the Federal Police and after that well it was academic; sixteen states in eight hours and with less damage than any other war that had taken place on U.S. soil.

Washington D.C. seemed to be the only place not completely under siege, but it was completely surrounded. The Black Wolves had taken every city surrounding it within the first four hours effectively trapping them there. They did hit military targets which was not shocking. This war was being prosecuted by a man who was only God knows how old and the first rule of war is to take down the enemy military. After that they could pretty much do whatever they wanted. Apparently, The Immortal wanted them to watch the nation it had taken 274 years to build be taken apart like as if it was little more than a sandcastle. All while U.N.N news teams were given free rein to broadcast it for all to see.

After twelve hours Timothy had seen enough, he stands up from his seat in the War Room. The place is quieter than he had ever thought possible. As he looked around the table no one even looked up to meet his eyes. Every head was down or up staring at nothing. Ten more states had officially been marked as lost and it was obvious that it was truly nothing, they could do to stop this. The Immortal had been playing with them that first week taking his time in order to give them a chance to surrender. Instead, they thought they could do what they had always done. Only this time they were not the biggest dog in the fight, and they were facing a wolf who already had them by the throat before the fight even started. Timothy puts his cap on and walked towards the elevator. The two soldiers he had adopted as his bodyguards and his aide Wu Yun all fell in with him. He followed the President's lead and did not say a word as they got into the elevator and left the War Room. Before the door closed, he saw his home state of Louisiana turn from red to black on the huge tactical screen.

The walk through the Pentagon was a somber one as the hallways and corridors were almost totally empty. Papers, folders, and boxes covered the floor where they were dropped when the people carrying them suddenly decided to quit their jobs and go home to their families. Timothy could not blame them this place no longer had any power and anyone who thought it did was a fool.

They reached a security checkpoint and found three armed Marines still there. They all turned from the news report playing on a wall tv and gave him a salute. Timothy returned it lazily and at that moment he realized how tired he was of fighting. These three Marines were younger than his own kids and here they were holding their post. He had no doubt that if the Black Wolves did attack these three would lay down their young lives to defend him and the other useless leaders they had sworn to serve and protect.

"All three of you go home now." Timothy says. "You are hereby relieved of duty and discharged from the United States military."

They all looked at him dumbfounded and none of them moved.

"That is an order Marines and so is this." he paused and looks each of them in the eyes. "If the Black Wolves come you do not fight them. You obey and you live your lives. The United States has fallen, and there will be a new government soon. Do not sacrifice yourselves for a flag that no longer means anything."

He stood silently watching the three of them. After a full minute of looking confused two of them unslung their guns and put them on the floor. They turned and walked away, breaking into a full run when they got past the set glass security doors. The third Marine remained and stared at General Sparks. He is a young black man and a smile slowly spreads across his face.

"Much respect General Sparks." says the Marine. "The Immortal and the Tide thank you for seeing reason."

One of his bodyguards moves to raise his gun. But Timothy puts out his hand and stops the soldier.

"As I told the Marines there is no point in laying down your life anymore."

Timothy looks at the young soldier and sees the fire in his eyes, it is the same fire he once had in his own. Today had extinguished that flame entirely. He turns his attention back to the smiling Black Wolf.

"Enjoy your life in the new world. Believe me, you will not regret your choice."

That is when it hit General Timothy Sparks, He had just betrayed his country by issuing his last orders to the Marines. He had told them to abandon their post and put themselves before their country. He felt his eyes begin to sting and then he felt a hand on his shoulder. He looks around and sees his aide of three years Staff Sergeant Wu Yun smiling at him also.

"It is ok sir it really is." Wu says. "In the end, the Tide will prevail, and The Immortal will establish a new world government. Choices will have to be made and you have made yours. Go home and be with your family. Spread the word and encourage everyone you know to make the same choice."

Timothy looks at the Asian soldier, a man that he had trusted for years now. He knew he should feel betrayed in that moment finding out a man that had ate dinner with his family and who Timothy considered a friend was really a sleeper agent in the group that was currently tearing his country apart. But, instead, he felt an incredible sense of relief.

"Let's get you home sir."

"Traitors!" yells the soldier he had stopped from raising his weapon earlier.

The soldier steps back and raises his rifle aiming directly at Timothy's head. The gun is an older pre-electronic model and in that moment all Timothy can see is the barrel aimed at his face. Then there is a boom and Timothy closes his eyes expecting to feel the bullet slamming into his head and making the darkness permanent. But he doesn't feel anything and when he opens his eyes, he sees the young man lying on the floor in a spreading pool of his own blood. He slowly looks to his right and sees his other bodyguard with his smoking rifle still held at his shoulder.

"Wrong choice my friend." the bodyguard lowers his rifle and nods to Timothy. "Let's get you home General."

Timothy just nods and lets the two men walk him out of the Pentagon for the last time.

CHAPTER 10

Tyanna lets out a scream of pleasure and digs her polished yellow fingernails into my chest hard enough to leave marks. The pain doesn't even register as I look up at the beautiful woman currently riding me. I admire the way her sweat-drenched chocolate skin shines in the light of the full moon. She is bouncing up and down on my steel hard cock and her beautiful breast mimic the motion. Not being able to resist any more I suddenly sit up and take one of her diamond hard nipples in my mouth. At the same time, I wrap one of my muscled arms around her waist holding her still while I begin to thrust up into her. It doesn't take long for her orgasm to hit and she wraps her arms around my neck and screams into my shoulder as her body shakes.

We have been going for what seemed like hours and I can tell she is almost done. She had already had over a dozen orgasms from penetration and six from oral. I had five myself but I never got tired so I could literally go on like this forever. She ended up lasting another fifteen minutes before she tapped me on the arm in submission. I am on top of her, so I raise up onto my knees and slide out of her. She lets out a moan as I leave her and then smiles up at me with her eyes closed.

"You know before you I have never tapped out to a man in my life." she says in a husky satisfied voice. "You are fucking amazing and that thing is dangerous."

I smile and kiss each toe of both of her feet before removing her legs from my shoulders. She sighs and turns over on her side getting comfortable. I step out of the bed and lean in close to her ear. I kiss it gently and she squirms as she giggles.

"Can I get you anything love?" I whisper into her ear.

"I am fine babe." she whispers back.

I stand and cover her up, giving her one last kiss before I go into the bathroom. After a shower I pull on a pair boxers and shorts. Tyanna is sound asleep when I leave the bedroom. I am not surprised to find Zephrah waiting in the kitchen I had felt her presence about fifteen minutes before. She is eating a sandwich and smiles up at me when I walked past her to the fridge.

"That poor woman. I don't know if I should feel sorry for her or jealous." Zephrah says as she pops a grape in her mouth.

"I am pretty sure you aren't jealous since you are usually doing the same thing to the females you take to bed."

I pull out a bottle of water and take a long drink. I flick her ear as I walk past her into the living room.

"Ouch, asshole."

I chuckle and roll over the back of the couch and then sit back in it with my bare feet up on the still coffee table.

"So, what is the latest report?" I turn on the tv and pick a streaming service.

"Every major military base in the mainland United States has been captured." Zephrah begins as she finishes her sandwich. "Thirty-five states at now flying the Black Flag and the rest should be ours by the end of tomorrow. I sent out a stand-down order so our people can get some rest or else they would most likely be ours by morning. It'll give the opposition more time to consider surrender as well."

I can hear the annoyance in her voice as she said that last part. One reason I know that I have no mind control over the Blooded is the fact that Zephrah can still be annoyed by my way of doing things. After thousands of years, the only thing I know about the effects of my blood is that it connects to those who ingest a drop of it as children. Through this connection they seem to grow up with an ingrained understanding or my life's work and strong loyalty to me even though many have never met me. Though many have told me that they have met me many times in their dreams. I won't lie this has disturbed me and I have thought of ending the practice many times. I don't want to replace one chain with another, that is just not the world I am trying to build. But I have had many conversations with my Blooded followers over the millennia and they all gave me the same answer: They do not feel chained or enslaved if anything they feel freed and focused.

They see the world with the clarity of an immortal who has witnessed every kind of cruelty humanity is capable of but also every type of kindness. It is an understanding they feel I should share with the entire human race. That idea is one I have serious misgivings about. I did not want to promise freedom and equality and then force people to give their newborns my blood. If it were going to happen it would have to be a voluntary choice, but the question was did I want that? If I am being honest with myself the question would be can, I stop it? As I said before my blood has been passed around for millennia within families all over the world. It only takes a drop within twelve hours of birth and someone would be connected to me for the rest of their lives. It is terrifying to think of the entire world being connected to me one day, but I opened a box I could no longer close the day I shared my blood.

I pull myself back to the present, "Good then we can begin phase two of the plan." I pick a zombie movie and hit play. "Putting the new government and economic system in place. Has President Deckland settled into the Area 51 bunker?"

"Gift wrapped in about fifty tons of concrete and under guard by what is left of the Secret Service and military loyalist." she sits on the arm of the couch. "I hear they have even been pulling as many non-electronic weapons out of storage as possible. They seem to be ready to make a fight of it."

"Well, all we can do is hope that they see reason." I truly mean it I don't want to see so many lives lost for an idiot like Gerald Deckland. "By the time we are ready to unwrap that gift perhaps they will have seen reason and abandon the little worm. We will be dealing with more immediate issues very soon. The patriots, rebels, terrorists, and flat-out racists. I absolutely can't wait until the resistance is formed and they start painting the red, white, and blue on the side of buildings. Though it's the more radical groups I am worried about."

"We have been accessing the government databases." she pulls out a tablet and passes it to me. "You would be surprised how detailed their records are on the various hate groups and radicals in the country. This list goes on for fifteen pages with twenty names on each and that is just the west coast. I have subtly increased our presence in those areas. If they make a move well, they shall learn the same lesson we have been teaching again and again for over a week now. They can either keep their hate to themselves or they can take their complaints directly to whatever god they believe in. We will make sure the trip is first class. And don't you worry we will make sure to ask them to surrender first."

CHAPTER 11

In Louisiana inside the Kisatchie National Forest is the fortified compound of the white supremacist group the Children of White Pride. The twenty acres of land was bought from the Louisiana government by the group during the 2034 Recession. The compound is the groups home and training ground with a hundred members of the group living there full time. With the country falling under the control of the Tide nearly every member in the state was now living within the compound. So, the current population currently over five hundred men, women and children. Nearly everyone is armed and ready to repel any invasion.

Randy Nichols the leader of the group sits in the compound meeting hall surrounded by his white brothers and sisters watching in disbelief as the reporters on television declares that America has fallen. The Black Flag of the Tide now flies over nearly every city in the country. The Black Wolves and their army of robots walk the streets, and the President along with nearly every other government official has either went into hiding or have just acquiesced to the demands of the terrorist. Randy feels his anger boiling over as all around him his people's reactions range from rage to horrified disbelief. Beside him his wife Holly begins to cry while his other wife Samantha holds her. Randy just covers his eyes with his hands.

It had been a week and a half since all this started and America had been not only crippled but conquered by a nigger and his group of mud people and race traitors. It had been the fate the Children of White Pride and groups like them had been trying to prevent for years. Over the last few decades, it had seemed like they were making progress but now he saw just how foolish they had been. He moves his hands and looks up at the Confederate and Nazi flags hanging on the wall on either side of the television and he feels his rage turn to patriotic passion. He stands to his feet and walks to the front of the room.

All eyes turn to him as he picks up his gavel and bangs it three times on the big oak podium that stands there. Once he is sure everyone is looking at him, he makes a slashing motion with his hand across his throat. The television is immediately switched off, and the room is silent. Randy reaches down and pulls out the signature mask he used to protect his identity when he did broadcast. He puts it on and then he pulled out what they consider the true American flag. It is exactly like the false one except for the black swastika and 11 stars representing the Confederate States. Randy drapes himself in it and looks up at all of his people. They are all on their feet giving him the Nazi salute.

"Sieg Heil!" Randy yells as he snaps off a perfect salute in return.

"Sieg Heil!"

The words echo off the walls of the meeting hall and rattle the windows. Randy shouts it again and again until the group is yelling it back at him over and over with no prompting. He closed his eyes and drank it in letting their pride fuel his. This was the war they had spent generations preparing for. Now, it was his time to send out the call and lead the push to take back first Louisiana and then the rest of the country. If all true members of the Aryan race came together, they could overthrow the so-called Immortal and his army of vermin. Bryson Kane's lies would be exposed, and Randy planned on being the man to take his head. After that, his name would be cemented in Aryan history alongside Adolf Hitler, Richard Baer, and Klaus Barbie. When he opens his eyes, he looks up as the camera drones float into position over the room and he knows his production team is waiting for his signal. He takes a breath and nods at the camera closest to him. The light goes from red to green signaling that he is live.

"Hello, my fellow white Americans I come to you today as together we experience the darkest day in not only the history of our country but in the history of our race." Randy says, the mask disguising his voice so that it was deeper and more powerful. "Many of you don't know me. I am known as the True Son and I am the leader of the Children of White Pride. The government and media have demonized us going as far as to label us a hate group and domestic terrorist. But all we have ever done is spread the truth. We warned you that the niggers, spics, chinks, and Jews were planning to turn white men, women, and children into slaves. We are the race that built this country and we have just watched it taken away from us by some nigger with a god complex. I for one will not stand for it, my brothers and sisters. Our so-called leaders have all went into hiding while you are left cowering in your homes waiting for the savages to come and have their way. They will put the men in chains and rape the women forcing them to bare more abominations into our world. Well, we will not stand by while this happens. We will fight for the rights of the Aryan race and retake our country. We will make America great again and-"

"That will be quite enough Mr. Nicholas." says a deep voice with a heavy southern accent from above Randy's head.

Randy spins around and sees a man's face on the television screen. He has heavily tanned skin and wears his long black hair loose so that it frames his face. His eyes are a deep icy blue and his face is hawk-like. He is sitting on a desk in an office and he wears a black suit of combat armor marking him out as an Elite of the Black Wolves. Randy knows this from the news reports that he had been watching.

"Boy, I swear I have heard a lot of bullshit in my time, but you really know how to pile it on son." says the Elite. "But I have gotten ahead of myself I apologize my name is Jon Luc LaCour and I am the new Governor of Louisiana."

"I wasn't aware that an election was held." Randy says regaining his voice finally. "So, I do not recognize your illegal-"

"Randy seriously just shut up." the authority in the Governor's voice absolute. "Didn't you say we would enslave and rape people? Do you believe that savages like us care about the law? No, according to what you believe mud people are not even smart enough to understand laws. But I am really not here to argue with you, Randy. I am here to tell you that you and your friends are more than welcome to run around and play soldiers in the woods and talk to each other about how the world belongs to white people until you all drop dead. But what you will not do is force your ignorance on the rest of the world. So, consider this your last broadcast. We are watching your every move and if you decide to not heed this warning well our next conversation with be face to face and we will be putting you in the dirt, not in chains."

Jon Luc glares at Randy and then his gaze shifts to the rest of the Children in the meeting hall.

"If you want to spend the rest of your lives listening to fools like Randy Nicholas then you are free to do so that is your right. But know that if you decide to follow him and attempt to hurt those who have chosen to accept change then the Black Wolves will show you no mercy. If you want to leave your hate behind and decide to rejoin society then you will be welcomed back with open arms. Housing, food, basic necessities, entertainment, and medical care are now free. All you have to do is report to the nearest shelter to be assigned a living space or simply return to your homes. It is your choice but if you live amongst us you will live under our laws. If you can't accept that I suggest you stay away."

Jon Luc looks back at Randy and is silent as if waiting for Randy to speak. But Randy was both fuming and terrified at the same time. He had thought he had the nerve to stand up to anyone he saw as a threat to his race but standing there under the gaze of a man who had helped to conquer the most powerful nation on Earth, he found himself unable speak. Jon Luc shakes his head as he stands up from the desk.

"I am a busy man Mr. Nicholas so do me a favor and don't add yourself to the list of things I need to take care of." Jon Luc says as he walks towards the camera. "Believe me you are not ready for the hell I will unleash on you. Go play dress up, burn a cross or just kill yourself loser. You would be doing the world a favor."

He walks off screen and then the television goes black. A few seconds later the camera drones all short out and fall to the floor. Randy slowly turns around and removes his mask. He looks up into the eyes of his people and for once in his life he has absolutely nothing to say. He lets the flag fall to the floor along with the mask as he walks out of the meeting hall.

Doctor Vivian Gordon is not a happy woman as she arrives in Jacobson Park in Lexington, Kentucky. The place was once the sight of a newly built shelter but now looked like a picture straight out of hell. Three suicide bombers posing as homeless people had walked in and blew themselves up taking dozens of innocent people with them. A medical team was already on site doing all they could which was quite a lot. With the Immortal making every piece of next generation technology available to them many of the victims who would otherwise have died before, they could ever be taken to a hospital, were given a chance to live. Two medics rushed past her with a badly wounded woman in a transparent stasis pad. They get her into the back of a medical speeder and take off.

Vivian has brought every doctor, nurse, medic and student with at least a week of hands on experience that UK Albert B. Chandler Hospital could spare along with her. She had just finished a surgery when she got the call. As the Chief Surgeon of the hospital, it was not hard for her to round up as many people as she had and get there. She gave everyone their orders and watched them all fan out and get to work helping who they could. Then she looked around for her husband. The entire area was now surrounded by Black Wolves and their robots. It did not take her long to spot her husband Leon Gordon and she speed-walked towards him. Her stride faltered; however, when she saw the five bodies he was standing over. All of them wore the black and camouflage uniforms of Black Wolves.

"Oh, God" she whispered under her breath.

Vivian slowly approaches her husband and puts a hand on the shoulder of his Elite armor. He looks down at her and she can see the fury and pain in his eyes. Before all this started Leon had been a therapist and she had only seen him this mad once before: When he heard about the Portland Massacre.

Vivian is a Converted Black Wolf and Leon is a Blooded. He is connected to every other Blooded making every one of them like family to him. Vivian wondered how many of the dead and wounded shared that connection. She could not imagine the pain this caused him. She had learned about all of this on her wedding night. Leon and she had dated for three years before that and she remembered thinking he was crazy back then, until he showed her the truth of it. Even after that, it took her years to accept it fully. They had three children and she had allowed him to blood them all. They were all spread across the world now fighting for the vision of The Immortal. But here and now stood the strongest man she knew, completely heartbroken. She reached up and pulled him down into a hug. He doesn't struggle and the tears begin to flow freely from both their eyes. They stay like that for minutes before she finally lets him go. His dark cheeks shine with tears but there is no shame there.

"What happened Leon?"

"They came in wearing clothes lined with SX-6." Leon says in a flat voice. "It's liquid C-4 it is just as stable and more powerful. It is illegal in almost every country because it is almost completely undetectable until it is about to explode. We have the whole thing recorded as the videos uploaded after death. They came here specifically for the security force everyone else was collateral damage. We usually don't post combat robots at these sites because we want people to feel welcome. Their scanners are next gen, and they could have detected the explosives. I had seven stationed here, two were rushed off to the hospital already. They were far enough away from the blasts for their shields to do some good."

She knew this was a war, but she didn't expect this level of atrocity. She looked around at the bodies of men, women, and even children who had come here because they were promised food, medicine, and a bed to sleep in. Instead, they were slaughtered, and they were not even the intended targets. She watched as a young student nurse stumbles away from a small badly burned boy and falls to his knees to throw up. Vivian's face hardens as she goes into the clinical mindset all veteran doctors have to develop. She looks back at Leon and points to the child who is being covered with a sheet.

"Whoever did this doesn't get to live Leon." the venom in her voice surprises her husband. "They do not get to keep breathing after this. There can never be peace in the world when people who are capable of this are in it. So, you find them, and you remove them like the cancers they are."

Vivian had taken an oath to protect life but if she had the chance, she would cut the hearts out of the people responsible for this. Leon looked his wife in the eyes and nodded before he activated his helmet and faceplate hiding his face behind the red-eyed mask.

"They don't get to live." he said his voice now cold and machine like.

Vivian turns and takes a deep breath before she walks away to do her duty.

In a bunker underneath Oxford Farm outside Lexington, Kentucky Dr. Melvin Watts watches the news report playing on one screen and the feeds from the hacked cameras in the area surrounding Jacobson Park. His experiment had been a stunning success and now he watched the aftermath. The news reports were amazingly accurate proving that this new government was much more forthcoming than the one it had replaced. Melvin made a note of that with his robotic hands flying over his dual holographic keyboards. His cybernetic eyes shifted from one screen to the next making observation while his genius mind processed the information.

Around him, his team worked just as fast as him watching the news reports about other probing attacks happening around the country. All of them were heavily modified like Melvin himself and all of them are geniuses in the world of cybernetics and hacking. To the rest of the world, the people in this underground facility are all dead. Greyware is a top-secret project devoted to devising unconventional strategies to deal with America's enemies. Strategies that would not normally be used due to trivial limitations like morals, ethics, or concern for human life.

Melvin had just blown up 134 people in order to test out the limitations of the Black Wolves shield technology. He had done this by activating a terrorist sleeper cell that had been embedded in the states by the Chinese government years ago. The suicide bombers had all had control chips embedded in their brains. He had hacked the Chinese database earlier that year and had their names, records, and access codes. Activating them and sending them orders had been simple since he could send the orders directly to the chips. They each had stockpiles of weapons and equipment so that wasn't an issue. The biggest hurdle had been getting them from all over the country to the target location. That had taken insane coordination and 96 straight hours without sleep on Melvin's part. Between the bumbling of government forces and the surgical percussion of the Tide, it had pushed even his genius intellect to its limits. Even with all his efforts only a little over half of them arrived when he needed them.

When all this first started the group had been ordered to begin their work on a strategy to defeat the Tide. They started off like they always did by trying to hack the networks of Black Tide. They had put backdoors into the massive company's network as they did to every major company in the world. So, they had expected to be able to get in with relative ease and start the process of cutting Bryson Kane's knees from under him. But, instead of finding open doors, they found the most sophisticated security network they had ever seen. It was the next generation in every way with ever-shifting codes, firewalls within firewalls, and some of the most vicious viruses they had ever seen. They had actually lost two members of their team as viruses leaped from their computers into their cybernetics. Melvin had watched with fascination as Daniel Lukes had been melted from the inside out as his cybernetics were forced to overheat. Mary Stains suffered a dual heart attack as both her real heart and artificial one seized up. After that, they realized that this was not going to be simple at all. They did not expect things to get so bad so fast. The country had fallen in less than two weeks and Bryson Kane revealed himself to be Immortal in not only name but in body. The team was divided on how this was possible. Some thought it was a hoax and others thought it was a new form of technology. Melvin is a part of the latter group and he wants more than anything to get his hands on that tech.

Now, that they no longer had anyone to report to Grayware was operating on their own and working towards their own goals. They first needed to find a weakness and then exploit it. Melvin believed that he had already done that. He watched as the Black Wolf wearing the armor of the Elites stood crying over the bodies of his fallen as he hugged the woman doctor. Their weakness is their emotions and compassion. Their emotions overrode their logic and that would be their downfall.

Melvin started typing furiously as he sent orders out to other members of the Chinese sleeper cell. They are positioned in Baton Rouge, Louisiana. He was going to see how the Wolves reacted when their leadership was decapitated. He pulled up a still of Jon Luc LaCour taken from the interrupted white supremacist broadcast and he sent it off to the agents with a single order attached: Kill by any means.

After that he returned his attention to his other project. He pulls up the screen showing a classified file detailing an Area 51 project called Archfiend. The deeper Melvin dug into the Project the more fascinated he became. He smiles as he begins to hack deeper into the Area 51's network.

Jon Luc stands at the top of the tower of the Louisiana House of Representatives. He was looking at nothing in particular just taking a moment to himself. The easy part was over, and the state belonged to the Tide. Now, came the reform and that would not be easy. Louisiana had been a neglected state for a very long time. Known mainly for New Orleans and food it is a place people only want to visit not live. Those who are born here will often do anything to get out. The state is and always has been run by old-money families. Families who had been around since the Confederacy and had helped them in their efforts to keep Louisiana a slave state. Jon Luc doesn't come from money; he is a Cajun that grew up in the Acadiana swamps. In his youth he traveled with and studied under The Immortal to became one of his Elites but when given the chance he came back home to live amongst his people once again.

Now, Louisiana had been given to him to govern by The Immortal and he considers it the greatest task of his life. He had already selected his Regents and set The Immortals reforms in motion. He had shut the state down allowing people to be at home with their families during this time of change. Meanwhile the Black Wolves and their robot companions had taken to the streets to either offer a helping hand or dole out controlled violence. There had been deaths but only when absolutely necessary in accordance with the will of The Immortal. It would take time, but Jon Luc would see Louisiana prosper in his lifetime.

He looks to his left as another black armored figure lands on the tower. Her helmet and faceplate retract revealing the face of his oldest daughter Tonya. She isn't smiling as she approached him, and Jon Luc knows he will not like the news she brings.

"What happened?" Jon Luc asked.

"There have been several attacks around the country." Tonya says holding a tablet out to him. "These are some of the news reports."

Jon Luc takes it and watches the four news reports playing at once. A suicide bombing of a shelter in Lexington, Kentucky, fire bombings that gutted three apartment buildings in Boston, Massachusetts, a gas attack in a mall in Orlando, Florida and mass shooting of a church in Little Rock, Arkansas. All of the attacks claimed innocent lives which was horrifying but there true purpose was clear to him even before he flipped to the report sent from the HQ in Atlanta now known as the Tower of The Immortal among the Wolves. Someone was probing them looking for weaknesses and monitoring their responses. Jon Luc reads the report that came straight from The Immortal himself.

"We are most likely dealing with a shadow ops organization whose activities are not kept on easily accessed records. Our intel teams digging through the captured systems, but they may be capable of wiping their digital footprint. It is possible we are dealing with sleeper cells either trained domestically or foreign. The attacks are all attacks used to probing our responses and the weaknesses of our technology. This will escalate and they will come after leadership next. Be on the lookout for more weapons like SX-6 and possibly bioweaponry. The presence of Battlebots and drones will now be mandatory at all sites. They may scare people, but I would rather they be scared and alive. All Elites are ordered to remain in areas with as few innocents as possible. A list of individuals who will most likely be targeted has been attached. Stay vigilant, we will face this new threat and destroy it like the rest."

Jon Luc opens the attached file and scrolls down the list finding his name there pretty quickly.

"Well fuck if it's not one thing it's another." he says handing the tablet back to Tonya. "They are going fight us every step of the way and even go so far as to kill dozens of innocents just to get one real target."

"He said it would be like this." Tonya says meaning The Immortal. "He told us that no matter how cleanly we fought this war that innocent blood would be spilled. All we can do now is minimize that and eliminate the threats as fast as possible. If you are a target, then we use you to bait the trap."

Jon Luc looks at her and laughs. His daughter is all in for the cause and had been for the majority of her life. The majority of the LaCour family are Blooded and within their ranks are seven active Elites. Loyalty to The Immortal and dedication to his cause is engraved on their very DNA.

"Well shit Tonya do I get a last meal before you serve me up?" Jon Luc says his voice full of amusement.

"I will see if we have time for it in the schedule." Tonya retorts completely deadpan.

He was so proud of his daughter and always had been. In her normal life she had been one of the best lawyers in Louisiana, she had clawed her way to the top to earn that. She looked so much like his late wife Gloria that they could have been sisters. He had lost her in a car crash when Tonya was five. He had almost lost his daughter too since she had been in the car with Gloria that rainy night. Tonya had been badly hurt and the doctors had been ready to give up on her. Tonya had suffered brain and organ damage, but a new doctor arrived who turned out to be the best surgeon in the country at that time. He brought his own team and equipment. With no explanation as to why he had gotten on a jet and flown from Boston to Lafayette, he took over Tonya's care. At the moment Dr. Harry Lambert and Jon Luc met Jon had known why. Because family protected its own and Harry was Blooded as well, he had been sent by The Immortal. He not only saved Tonya but stayed with her throughout the long recovery process. He did all her surgeries after and helped her regain the ability to walk and speak. Today he and Jon Luc are still the best of friends and Harry now the Governor of New York is also on the list of likely targets.

"Like I always say you can catch anything with the right bait." he gives her a light kiss on the head. "So, let's bait the hook and see what nasties come up to take a bite."

Dai Hai used to be a massage therapist or at least he had pretended to be. Now he was what he was trained to be since childhood. Currently, he is in the city of Baton Rouge seeking his assigned target: Jon Luc LaCour. He made the journey from Scottsdale, Arizona abandoning his practice and his family without a second thought upon his activation. There he linked up with four others like himself and they have been holding up in a safe house watching and waiting.

In the back of his mind, Dai wondered if his family was okay. But it was like old memories there but not important. What was important now was completing his mission, it was the only thing in life that mattered anymore.

Dai is currently in Capitol Gardens blending in within the crowd of hundreds, all there to receive food and medical care. Most are the homeless from all over Baton Rouge, they disgusted Dai to his very core. People like them did not deserve help and in China, they would be put into work camps or simply killed. This new world would be a weak one and he intended to do what he needed to in order to help China put an end to it before it truly took hold. They would sweep the Tide from their homeland and then come to take America like they were always destined to. His current mission would most likely see everyone in the city of Baton Rouge dead but that was a small price to pay for a critical strike against these terrorists.

Dai forced himself not to grip the strap of his backpack not wanting to look suspicious as he moved through the crowd of human filth. The bomb he carried was known as China Special by American intelligence, it is filled with a nerve agent known as Silent Song. It is the deadliest substance ever created and this version was totally weaponized. Once set off it would spread 20 miles in every direction killing every living creature in the blast zone, then it would simply die itself.

They had tracked the target to the House of Representatives with ease. He had come on the news and gave a broadcast laying out the new laws and reforms that would be put in place in the coming weeks and months. They are weak laws that basically made everyone equal. Even those who worked their asses off to get ahead in life would be treated the same as those too lazy to get up off their asses. He truly hated America and all it stood for but even in China, a bum was a bum. His personal opinion of black people would have him labeled a racist. In China, they are considered plague carrying vermin like rats. They were widely blamed for the Covid-19 outbreak of 2020. In 2021 many had their citizenship or visa's revoked and were deported. Many of those still there were in prison where they belonged.

Dai reached his assigned location the memorial for Huey P. Long in the center of the Gardens. He stood pretending to read it but really, he was surveying his surroundings. Seeing that none of the bums were close enough to overhear him he taps the side of his shades activating the comm embedded inside his cap.

"Red 3 in position." Dai says before deactivating the comm.

He was the fifth to report in and at 6:00 pm they would all detonate. They were all moving into different positions in order to surround the House of Representatives and make sure that escape was impossible. Dai pulls out his phone and checks the live news feed showing the Jon Luc was still broadcasting from inside the building. He nods and then changes the phone to the camera app and swiping it over to the video setting. The red button in the center looked innocent enough but when he hit it the China Special would be detonated. He checks his watch, and it reads 5:55 pm.

Dai realized at that moment that he was five minutes away from death. He suddenly felt sad that he had not said goodbye to his wife Meng or his daughter Yao. He was idly considering sending them a message when a hand appeared on his wrist and then squeezed. The sudden burst of pain as his wrist was crushed was so intense that his hand opened reflexively, and he dropped the phone. An involuntary scream of pain came from his mouth. He watched through pain hazed eyes as someone stepped in and plucked the phone from the air. His training kicked in and he reached back to pull the manual detonation cord disguised as a large keychain. Before his hand made it halfway his other arm was caught, and he was taken to the ground. It was a soft takedown expertly done and it told Dai they knew what he was carrying. But he was not defeated yet since the bomb was also connected to a heart monitor and if his heart stopped it would still go off. Just as he bit down hard crushing the Silent Song filled capsule hidden in a false tooth, he saw the blue force field go up around him and the two holding him. He realized they were robots when the holographic disguises that made them look like bums failed. As his inside liquified and his skin melted from his rotting bones Dai Hai realized that they had been tricked. A half-second after his death the China Special went off and the toxic white smoke filled the force field.

Tonya LaCour watches as the white smoke filled the bubble force field in the center of Capitol Gardens. All around her Black Wolves and robots dropped their holographic cloaks as the signal for the end of the operation was broadcast. It had been a total success with all five suspects stopped. They even managed to capture one alive near the Claiborne Building.

To be honest Tonya was shocked that the trap worked so well but she supposed controlling the city and having access to everything was the defining factor. In the end, it had been the sleepers who gave themselves away. Tonya had ordered that every signal in the city be shut off except for the comms the Black Wolves used and broadcast node. Everything else was shut down or heavily suppressed. So, when five satellite-linked comm signals started transmitting it was like the sleeper had fired signal flares. From there it was just about drawing them into the trap. Her father had planned a broadcast anyway and the area around the House of Representatives had the least number of innocents. The Wolves moved in quickly, quietly moving any innocents from the area as they set up.

Things had gotten a bit tense when the chemical weapons were detected. Her people almost started foaming at the mouth when the chemical signature was identified as Silent Song. If even a whiff of that got into the air it would be a disaster. But she had held them all back and the operation went off without a hitch. She still had the entire area scanned by drones and bots though. They could not afford to do anything half-assed. She is in her full Elite armor with helmet and faceplate on. She blink-clicks a channel open to her wife Queenetta LaCour who was in the operation center located inside the House of Representatives.

"All known targets accounted for and chemical agent fully contained." Tonya says into the comm. "Are their signs of any further threats?"

"None that we can see Sweetie." Queenetta replies her deep southern accent even more pronounced over the comm. "I am widening the search, but we have no more rogue signals and no unknown chemical signatures showing up on the scanners. I have launched a drone with an Anti-Agent missile just is the case set to fire automatically if anything is detected but I am going to call this one clear love."

Tonya let out a breath of relief and the knowledge that they had an Anti-Agent missile on hand helped. The Anti-Agent is one of Black Tide's greatest creations, it was developed in the 2030s when chemical warfare had spiraled out of control. It was designed to clear air of toxic chemicals using replicating nanobots that would seek out and destroy the chemicals. The nanobots also inhabited the bodies of those inside its range and temporarily enhanced their bodies immune systems so that they could survive until the chemicals are destroyed and they could receive medical help. If the victims hadn't been exposed directly or for too long, they could survive the attack. With chemical weapons like Silent Song though they could only hope to stop the spread anyone exposed would be dead within seconds.

"Thank you, darling, keep me informed even it looks like nothing."

"You got it Sugar, you be safe out there and come home to mama." she blows her wife a kiss over the comm before clicking off.

Tonya smiles under her faceplate no matter what the situation her wife never changed. It's one of the main reasons she loved Queenetta so much. She fully planned on going home but first she had a prisoner to interrogate. Someone was pulling the strings on all this and she planned on seeing their head on a spike before she relaxed for a second.

"We are clear for now everyone but stay alert." Tonya says through her helmet speakers as she activate her grab-jet flight systems. "Report back to assigned areas to stay alert and ready. We will be in quick reactions status until further notice. Great work today Wolves."

She rises a few feet into the air and then puts her fists into the air and takes off heading towards the Claiborne Building.

As the hours passed the members of Greyware became more and more nervous as slowly one by one, starting with Melvin's operation in Baton Rouge, their operations went dark. They were not all using sleeper agents like him but the ones that were are the first ones to go dark.

It had started when Melvin's sleepers did not execute their orders at 6 p.m. He was watching as Jon Luc was being interviewed and had expected to see him melt on live tv along with most everyone in Baton Rouge. When that did not happen at the assigned time, he had tried sending orders to his agents and ran through the data feed to see if he could ascertain what happened to them. He tried to access the cameras around the House of Representatives area only to find that he was completely locked out. The same airtight cybersecurity they had encountered when trying to hack Black Tide was now covering the entire cyber network of Baton Rouge. He could not even hack a cellphone if it ran on the city Wi-Fi.

After that everyone's projects simply went dark. One by one they were kicked out of city networks as the cybersecurity program they had started calling Blackfire was added to every city and town network controlled by the Tide and this wasn't just in America but all over the world if they controlled it then it became totally impenetrable by outside hackers. Melvin wasn't even sure if he could hack a system running Blackfire if he were jacked directly into it.

By 10 pm all of their operations were dead, and the entire team was in a state of logical panic as they worked to pack up everything, they could so they could evacuate the bunker. It was very orderly but very rushed by their standards. They backed up all their data and packed the drives into cases before purging and then setting the self-destruction time. They had five minutes to get out before the thermite bombs planted on every piece of electronic hardware. The place would be nothing but slag afterward. They all got into separate elevators that led to different evacuation points on the surface.

Melvin steps out of the elevator into one of the horse stables. He expected to find members of the security team there waiting for him. They all posed as workers on the farm and were not allowed to come down into the bunker. The team never had much contact with them, and Melvin wondered had anyone checked on them since this all started. He had not but surely someone had. It was protocol when the evacuation process was activated for two members to meet each of them with a vehicle ready but all he found waiting for him were horses in their stalls.

"Useless meat bags." Melvin says under his breath as he picks up his cases and walks towards the stable doors.

Melvin had gone through so many cybernetic enhancements that he barely considered himself human anymore. It had all started when he lost his legs in a car crash. He had been given new cybernetic ones and he realized how superior they were to his old ones. So, he had his arms replaced and then his eyes. It went on and on until he became what he is now a cyborg and one of the United States government's most dangerous black hat hackers. Though since there was no United States anymore that last part was irrelevant.

He reached the door and kicked it open expecting the find the guards waiting out there. They were in fact there and so was the car. Both guards were on the ground beside the car at the feet of a black armored, red-eyed figure leaning against it.

"So, you are what a terrorist looks like these days." the Elite says in a voice made machine cold by the helmet and faceplate. "An asshole who needs power tools to take a shit."

Melvin drops his cases and takes a step back. How had they found this place? When it was obvious that the country would fall, they had activated the info destroyer they had embedded into the government network. It deleted every trace of their existence on record. Less than a dozen people knew enough to lead anyone to this location or the locations of any of their bunker and even the President himself wasn't counted in that number. Melvin's mind was traveling in several directions at once when the Elite spoke again.

"We found you by tracing the command signal you were blindly sending to the control chip of your captured sleeper in Baton Rouge. From there we located the stealth satellite network and we proceeded to backtrack all signals sent to that satellite. Took our people about two minutes to break your encryption and get past the Grayware firewalls. But to your credit they did say it was the finest piece of shit coding they had ever faced. That is high praise coming from those nerds so you should feel honored. From there we just watched and learned. We proceeded to shut you down piece by piece until finally, we got to the core."

Melvin's mind was spinning now. If what the Elite said was true, he had been the one to lead them here. They had followed him right back to the bunker like sharks trailing bleeding prey. He was one of the smartest men in the world and they had played him for a fool. His anger suddenly overrode his fear and with a mental command to his implants he activated the hidden weapons within his body. His right arm changed into a ray-gun and a blue laser blade deployed from his left. This was the first time he has had to use weapons outside of the test range and suddenly he found he was very fascinated to see what they would do to the Elite's armor and the body under it.

Melvin sets the ray-gun to full auto as he raises it locking onto the Elite. He opens fire and the intense blue laser bolts light up the night as the streak towards their target. Then the Elite moves and turned into a blur of motion. The first bolts bit the car cutting through it like it was made of paper. Melvin attempts to track him with the ray-gun but even with his cybernetic eyes and adaptive targeting system he is too slow. If he had any combat training at all he would have stopped firing and gotten his blade up. But he had not bothered with getting training, depending on his technology and intellect to give him the upper hand in any situation. It was this hubris that got him killed.

If he hadn't been such an egomaniac, he would have used his brain and all the data they had gathered that proved the Black Wolves used superior technology and their soldier are masters of combat. Melvin barely had time to register that he was about to die when the Elite appeared on his left side, ripped off his arm, and rammed the laser blade into the side of his neck. The blade punched out of the other side and he stopped firing the ray gun as critical damage warnings started to run across his vision. He struggled to breathe, and his mouth and face begin to spasm as his body truly began to register the catastrophic damage it had suffered. Then with a hard twist and yank the Elite removed Dr. Melvin Watts' head from his shoulders.

Leon Gordon stands over the body of the decapitated cyber-terrorist. He casually tosses the torn-off arm to the side. He had been chomping at the bit ever since they found the location of this place. But he had been patient as they coordinated with other cells to contain the threat. These maniacs had been set to cause untold destruction and take tens of thousands of lives all across the United State in order to gather information on the weaknesses of the Tide. All they had managed to do was escalate the speed and ferocity of the conquest. They had exposed not only themselves, but every group like them.

The Immortal had ordered all the seized information of the now overthrown United States government to be analyzed. That had revealed more clandestine operations within the country which he promptly ordered destroyed. There was no surrender offered to these people not after what Greyware had pulled. Normally Leon would not paint everyone with the same brush, but he had seen children die horrific deaths and held his brothers and sisters as they died. He was past compassion for any organizations that were capable of anything near what Grayware had done.

"They don't get to live." says Leon as he activates his grav-jet flight system and takes off.

The other members of Grayware and their security teams are all wiped out. Below the surface, the facility is turned to slag. The other Elites all join Leon in the air, and they get in formation and head back towards Lexington. Below them the vehicles of the cleanup team drive down the road towards the farm.

CHAPTER 12

The sticks rolled smoothly over the drum set as I played. Over the many years of my life, I have had many passions: hunting, sailing, sports, mountain climbing, and many more. But the one passion I have never lost interest in is drumming. From the African djembe to the twenty-four-piece set I am currently playing I have played drums all across the world, learning every style and evolution there is. The practice calms me and clears my mind. Currently, I am playing alongside Max who is playing guitar. We have been going for nearly 6 hours straight and we are both able to go another six without ever playing the same tone twice.

The second week was over, and the United States was officially conquered. Every state and territory now lived under the Black Flag. It was a feat once thought impossible, but the Tide had not only done it we made it look easy. With conquest came the changes I promised.

I officially abolished capitalism and replaced it with the one I called Evolved Free Market which basically meant everything was free. People were allowed to work if they wanted to, but they were not required to. Food, medicine, housing, and everything else were all provided to them free of charge. Black Wolves would move into positions of governance and management within the system and robots would become the labor force. Those who want to join the new government given the opportunity. Those who want to continue to run their own business or who want to start their own business under the new economic system can apply. They will be given all the resources they need and those who just want to lay around their houses, travel or pursue their individual passions are free to do that as well.

All children were encouraged to attend the schools where they would receive whatever level of education, they were comfortable with. The same was offered to those who wanted to attend college without having to sign away decades of their lives to pay back student loans.

I also completely reformed the entire legal system cutting it in half and then trimming it down even further. The cases of every prisoner were being reviewed and the prisons slowly emptied as those who didn't need to be there were released. Those who remain were to receive humane treatment and be offered real reform and if they did well their cases would be reviewed again, and they would be given the opportunity to rejoin society. The law enforcement community was also being rebuilt in much the same way. The files of former officers were being reviewed and those who were cleared would be called and offered retraining. If they accepted, they would attend academies and learn the Black Wolves way of doing things. It would be a year of training and psychological testing at the minimum and in the meantime, the law would be enforced by Black Wolves and their robot partners.

Then there were the churches most of whom believed I was the devil and would see them all burned to the ground. I had received phone calls, letters, and meeting requests from every representative of every religion up to and including the Pope. All of whom thought I would outlaw religion. I have no intention of doing anything of the sort. Taking away religion would leave a massive hole in the psyche of the world and that would have to be filled. Not to sound like an egomaniac but I have no interest in being a god. So, no I won't be outlawing religion. I will be outlawing the hateful, sexist, and downright inhumane practices that people do in the name of their religions and I have made that clear. I know this will not win me many fans and truthful I don't care. They can praise, worship, pray, and manifest until they are blue in the face I don't care. But if a little girl is burned because she shows her face in public or a boy is beaten because he loves another boy then I will care very much. I will take great pleasure in seeing those responsible go to see their respective gods sooner than they imagined they would.

I did not expect the change to be easy and America was only the first country of many it would have to be enacted in. Many other countries would need far more social and legal change before they were anywhere near acceptable.

Then there was the small matter of the President locked away in Area 51 with what remained of those loyal to him. Many of the troops guarding him had seen the writing on the wall and abandoned him. I had sent him many messages offering him a peaceful end to it all only to be ignored. I had received reports from my man inside that he was reaching out to leaders around the world requesting aid and getting turned down each time. They all knew that they were next and did not want to speed up the inevitable. Some like Britain and France had already reached out to me ready to negotiate a peaceful transition. While others like China and Russia were threatening nuclear strikes. To them, I helpfully suggested that they check and see if their nukes worked before threatening to use them. Spoiler alert I either deactivated every nuclear weapon on the world or had my people quietly move in and secure the launch sites.

I knew I had to go and drag Deckland out of that bunker. I had no real concerns about that until Zephrah burst into my studio breathing hard.

"What happened?" I asked. "Please don't say, zombies."

"Our agent in Area 51 is dead." she answered.

My good mood quickly fades and is replaced by pure rage, "How did he die?"

"From what I can tell it was something out of a sci-fi movie."

"Fuck my life." I drop my head. "What have these idiots done now?"

I put my sticks down and stand up from behind the drums. I walk over to her and see that she is holding a tablet. My interest is peaked I must admit, I hold out my hand and she gave me the tablet. On the screen, a video feed from the mask of my fallen Black Wolf Kevin McKenzie was queued up. I hit play and watched until it was over.

"It would seem I will need my armor." I pass the tablet back to Zephrah. "It looks like I have to clean up yet more white people shit."

CHAPTER 13

One hour earlier...

President Gerald Deckland sits in the conference room of the Area 51 bunker. He had been down there for a week watching as the country fell to the Tide. He watched the news broadcast as The Immortal and his Black Wolves gave speeches proclaiming the greatness of the world they were creating. All the while he had been calling every alley America had begging for aid only to be denied by one after the other. The satellite phone lay broken in a corner where he threw it after getting yet another rejection this time from the fucking Russians of all people. He had offered them the keys to America and only to be hung up on. All around the room what was left of the American government sits in silence no one daring to make eye contact with anyone else. They were slowly being abandoned by the military forces who put more value on finding their families than protecting their President and what was left of the lawful government of their nation. Even members of the Secret Service had abandoned them, though Zachary had tried to hide that from him by saying he had stationed them in different areas. The staff of the base had all been sent away before they had all arrived leaving only key personal behind.

"Maybe we should consider talking."

The words came from the end of the conference table and Gerald didn't even bother looking up to see who it was. The silence continued after that until another voice spoke up and this one, he recognized as Director Tracey Todd the head scientist of the secret facility.

"There is the Archfiend Project sir."

Gerald puts his hand over his eyes and closes them, he feels another migraine coming on. The fucking Archfiend Project is something even he did not have the stomach to think about. But she was very right they did have it and the fact that he was actually considering using it showed just how fucked they truly were.

"What is the Archfiend Project." asked Fred.

Gerald looked up at his Vice President and then down at Doctor Todd.

"You want to field that one, doc?" he asked the middle-aged woman at the end of the table.

She looked back at him and then stood up brushing some graying blonde hair from her face. All the eyes in the room turned to her and she gave them a winning smile. It made Gerald want to puke, she was actually proud of the monster they had created.

"I think it would be easier if I just showed you." Tracey says.

They all look at Gerald who just stands up and gestures for her to lead the way. She had been nagging him about this since they got there, and he had held his ground. But fuck it if Heaven won't open its gate, Hell is always ready to take their business. The others stand up and they all fall in behind Doctor Todd and the armed Secret Service agents. Fred fell in beside Gerald and leaned in to speak.

"What the hell is the Archfiend Project?" Fred asked his voice low.

"A deal was made with the Devil and Archfiend is the result." Gerald replies his voice flat. "I guess it's time to decide if I am going to be the President that has to pay up."

Tracey Todd has devoted her life to science and becoming the Director of Area 51 was the culmination of all her hard work. At 55 she has never been married and has no children; her work has been her life. She has worked on projects that have changed the world and when she was pulled from DARPA and offered Area 51, she did not hesitate.

The place was believed to house aliens and spacecraft thanks to years of misinformation fed to the public. In truth it is simply a research and development facility. What truly makes it special is they have absolutely no restrictions and a budget that is greater than that of the military. Some of the world's greatest inventions over the last 95 years have come from the work done here. They rarely took credit for it, they often sold it to a company or individual and in return they took a portion of the profit. The real reason barely anyone knew what happened within the facility is it takes little to no money from the government. That is the key to keeping a secret in America is don't ask for anything and still produces results.

When all of this started Tracey and her team had predicted that it would get bad but when the President actually called her and told her to activate the bunker she finally saw her chance to prove that one of the longest running projects Area 51 had undertaken was worth the years of work, money spent and lives lost. It was finally time to activate Archfiend and she could think of no better time.

      Ever since Bryson Kane had done his broadcast revealing his true nature to the world the only thing, she has thought about is how much they could learn by dissecting him. He is the next step in human evolution and the fact that he had hidden away all these years was a disservice to his entire race. There is also the possibility that he is not human at all in which case he would be the catalyst for the evolution of an entire race. Either way she planned on being the one to find out what makes him what he is, and she had no doubt that Archfiend could capture him for her. The only reason she had not already set it loose is the fact that she needs the code, DNA sample and retinal scan of the current United States President. It was a stupid protocol put in place after Archfiends first and only field use back in 1965 by Lyndon B. Johnson. Even though the operation was a complete and utter success the fact that they had lost control of the weapon was not looked upon favorably. The results of this loss was over 1500 deaths over the course of three days and one of the biggest joint cover-ups in history. It was just a repeat of what always happened and why humanity had not yet settled new worlds or eliminated diseases. A brilliant creation is locked away because it doesn't work as simple-minded people want it to the first time. People forget that if it were not for the work of doctors in the Nazi camps during World War Two modern medicine would have been set back by decades. All they saw was the death and not the breakthroughs that have saved the lives of many millions if not billions of others. There could be no gains without losses, that is a lesson the world has had to learn over and over. A lesson that they are learning yet again as Bryson Kane and his Tide forces it down their throats.

      The group moves through the bunker passing through the residential area. They don't see any of the family members that now call the bunker home. It's around lunchtime so they are most likely all in the cafeteria. Tracey had not been comfortable with the thought of more space being taken and resources being used up by people who were absolutely useless in their current situation. But the President would not take no for an answer, and even with the extra strain on their resources, they had enough food, water, and supplies to last them years.

      They arrive at an elevator with an I.D scanner, keypad, and DNA sampler. Tracey scans her I.D, puts in her code, and then puts her thumb into the DNA sampler. There is a prick and the lights above the elevator changed from red to green. The doors open and the inside of the elevator is spacious enough to hold up to twenty-four people comfortably. She steps to the side and ushers the others inside first, there is no argument from any of them. She steps into the elevator last and hits B9 which is one level lower than they are now. The doors close and the elevator starts to lower silently, then stops and dings. When the door opens a rush of chilled air meets them as they step into the controlled environment of the Archfiend Project bio lab. Tracey had officially released almost all of her staff keeping only those absolutely necessary to continue their most important research. Ten of her absolute best were waiting beside a table with a figure wearing only compression shorts lying on it. Tracey hears sharp intakes of breath from behind her as most of the group lays eyes on their magnificent creation for the first time.

"What is that thing?" Secretary of Defense Henry Blake asked.

Tracey instantly felt her anger rise and it took all herself control not to bite his head off. The being on the table was very much a man and he was of greater value to the world than a thousand bureaucratic boot lickers like Henry Blake could ever be. Tracey took in a calming breath before she spoke.

"He is a man Mr. Secretary, and his name was Norman Pope." Tracey says her tone icy. "During the Vietnam War, he was a Sergeant in the Green Berets. He fought for his country and never received a single medal for his actions. He broke into POW camps, and saved dozens of American lives, he-"

"He lost his fucking mind and started slaughtering innocent civilians for sport." President Deckland says cutting her off.

Tracey turned her glare on him, and he glared right back as he walked past her over to the table. He broke eye contact with her to look down at the man formally known as Norman Pope who was now known by his codename: Archfiend. The man no longer looked like he did when he was in Vietnam. His skin once white with a farmer's tan was now grey as a stormy sky and reptilian. His head once covered in long blonde hair was now bald. His frame once covered in bulky muscles from hours of weightlifting was now as lean as an Olympic runner. His fingers and toes are all tipped with black claws capable of slicing through steel as if it were paper. He was currently unconscious on the table with heavy restraint clamps over his chest, stomach and legs. So, no one could see his golden eyes that were capable of seeing in total darkness with perfect clarity. They also couldn't know that he is capable of hearing a pin drop in a hurricane or that he could track a smell over a hundred miles. As Norman Pope, he was trained as one of the best killers in the world. As Archfiend, he is the best predator in the world and quite possibly the next evolutionary step for humanity as a whole.

Of course, his evolution had been forced along faster than it would have happened in nature. But, even before years of gene therapy, bio and technological enhancement, and psychological retraining Norman Pope was already well on his way to being the next step in human evolution. He possesses twenty-four pairs of chromosomes and not the normal twenty-three. That extra set of chromosomes is often associated with Klinefelter syndrome which is more often found in males with only twenty-three complete pairs of chromosomes and one unpaired one giving them forty-seven. It is much rarer for someone to have twenty-four complete pairs giving them forty-eight. In many unfortunate cases, this leads to mental illness or slowed physical development, but in Norman's case, it was the exact opposite. He was naturally strong, faster, and smarter than many others. Though some would say his homicidal rages were a sign that he was yet another failure, Tracey saw it for what it was: A superior species proving its dominance over a lesser one.

"After he was found out, this man killed everyone who came after him and fled into the jungles of Vietnam." President Deckland continued. "Where he spent over two years hunting and killing everyone unlucky enough to cross his path. The special force that finally captured him lost over half their number in the process. Then instead of being put down like the rabid animal he is, he was given over into the custody of the brilliant minds of Area 51 who proceeded to turn a maniac into a killing machine. Then guess where they sent him for his first test."

He holds out hands to the group encouraging them to guess. Tracey clenched her jaw to keep silent and no one else spoke.

"Nobody?" his voice full of condescension. "Well let me tell you then, I mean it is a secret classified so high that I could have you all shot just for seeing this fucking monster. But what good are secrets without a fucking country?"

His voice was getting higher as he spoke, and he let out a laugh that was frankly scary.

"They sent him right back to Viet-fucking-nam!" he yelled. "It took him two years to capture him and they sent him right back to that godforsaken country to seek and destroy a Viet Cong leader and his entire cell. Believing that they could control this thing, that they had it fucking trained! Guess what the mission was a complete and utter success until that is, he got loose again and this time he wasn't just a trained killer he was an engineered one. 1,457 people dead in and around the city of Da Nang over the course of three days. It took three days and nearly ever Green Beret we had in country at the time to do it. It killed forty-three of them during that time, which actually makes its record 1,500 in three days. Want to know something that is even funnier, they did not even bring this thing down. It just fell asleep in the middle of the last village it slaughtered. That is what this monster you are so proud of is capable of and you fucking nutjobs have spent the past 85 years making him an even better killing machine. Now, you want me to put the code in to wake this walking nightmare in order to do what exactly?"

"Mr. President I think you need to calm-"

"Don't you fucking tell me to calm down, you crazy bitch!"

He walks over to one of his agents and pulls the man's sidearm from its holster. Everyone in the room steps away from him and the Secret Service agents have to fight the urge to aim their guns at the President of the United States. He walks back over to the table and jams the gun against the eye of the sleeping Archfiend. Tracey's heart skipped a beat and she saw Monica who is at the station monitoring Archfiend's vital signs go stiff. What happened next was so fast no one could have possibly stopped it.

"Answer the question Doctor Todd or I will blow this maniac's brains out here and-" the President started to yell the threat but never finished.

There was the sound of snapping metal and then President Deckland let out a scream of agony as Archfiend ripped his arm off his body. The scream did not last long because with one swipe of its black claws Archfiend decapitated President Gerald Deckland, sending his head flying across the room. Blood spread everywhere as the President's headless corpse simply fell to the floor with a sick thud.

The shock of the sudden and brutal murder froze everyone in place. Even the Secret Service agents who were trained to give their lives for the President stood in shocked horror. Archfiend was not frozen, and he wasted no time ripping what remained of his restraints off like they were made of paper. He then proceeded to follow his training and attacked the most immediate threats. Unfortunately for the Secret Service agents, their weapons made them slightly more dangerous than the rest. He was on the first one in the blink of an eye and the man was holding his guts in his hands as they poured from his open belly a second later. Archfiend tore through anyone in his way to get to his next target. The gunfire and screaming are what snapped Tracey out of her shock.

She looks to her right and watched as Archfiend ripped the arm off another agent. The finger of the man's severed arm still squeezed the trigger of his rifle and bullets spread around the room hitting several people and machines. Tracey watched the back of Vice President Fred March's head simply explode as a round punched out the back of it. She was sprayed with hot blood and brain matter as the Vice President fell. Then suddenly she was running towards the station where Monica had been moments before. When she reached it, she found the young woman was on the floor, a round had punched through her eye, and a pool of blood was slowly spreading around her head. Tracey spared this a moment's notice before she turns to the computer station. She navigated the holographic screen with quick flicks of her hands. She made it to the screen she was looking for, the one that would allow her to access the kill chip in Archfiend's brain. She tapped it but nothing happened, she tapped it again and again.

A message appeared in bright red letters, "You left us for dead, so we left a little gift for you. Hint: Your monster is awake."

Then she noticed that the screams had stopped behind her. The lab was dead silent except for the slow controlled breathing directly behind her. Tracey closed her eyes as the cold hand of fear gripped her very soul. She slowly turned around a movement that seemed to take an eternity. When she opened her eyes, she found herself looking into the golden eyes of Archfiend. She opened her mouth to speak but only blood poured out as a sudden pain in her chest made her look down. She sees Archfiend's hand was buried up to the wrist in her chest. She lets out a short laugh before he pulls it out and lets her fall to the floor dead.

Kevin McKenzie hates his job. He has to put his life on the line to protect a racist and that just doesn't sit right with him. But he is a Converted Black Wolf, and these are the orders he was given. As a white man, he had survived the purge of the Presidential Secret Service detail. It had been the most shameful display he had ever seen in his seven years on the job. Wayne Simmons had been in the service for fifteen years most of them spent on the Presidential detail. He had even taken a bullet for the previous President and how was he repaid? They offered him a desk job in the Treasury or early retirement. The man wasn't even a Black Wolf and would have given his life for the President even though he knew Deckland was a racist.

Now, here was Kevin sitting in the cafeteria guarding the family members of what was left of the Presidential cabinet. He watched as the First Lady Angela Deckland sat talking with the Chief of Staff Lana Andrews as they ate. He idly wondered if the First Lady knew she was laughing with her husband's mistress. The Chief of Staff had been excluded from most of the President's meetings lately, which was not shocking it wasn't much staff left to be chief of at this point. No more pissed off congressman and senators to keep in line and no political advise to give. The President is really just an empty puppet at this point and everyone there knew it. The Immortal and the Tide ran America now. Kevin couldn't wait to get this over with so he could rejoin his family in Colorado.

He was just thinking of his wife Stacy when his watch started to go nuts. He looks at it and sees that it is flashing red with the message: POTUS DOWN.

"What the fuck?"

He was already on the move with the other agents in the cafeteria. All of their watches are connected to the heart monitors of all their charges. What the hell had happened? The last report was the President, and the others were headed down to Sub-level 9. Director Richards is with them since the President had ordered him to lead the detail personally. Kevin grabs the First Lady and her children and started to rush them to their assigned safe space. Another agent Amy Spears was also assigned to them and she fell in front with her gun up leading the way. The comms were going crazy with people trying to get information. On top of that, the First Lady was stopping every few steps demanding answers. Finally, Kevin just started dragging her as they followed Amy.

"Let me go and tell me where my husband is now!" the First Lady yells.

Kevin ignores her pushing her up against the wall to get out of the way of the Marines Quick Reaction Force stormed past them going the other way. Amy did the same with the two kids and they held them there until the Marines passed. Then they kept moving until they reached the assigned safe room for the President and his family. The kids went in with no prompting, but Kevin had to shove the First Lady inside. Amy hit the flashing red button on the right side and the steel door slammed shut and locked. The room was filled with supplies and if no one came back within eight hours a door to a tunnel would open allowing them to leave and reach a safe point on the surface. With their charges secured the two agents turned and ran the same direction as the QRF.

His name is Norman Pope but that was not his name. His name is Archfiend but that sounds stupid. None of it matters all that matters is that he is starving. These are the thoughts going through the head of the thing that was once Norman Pope and is now known as Archfiend as he takes a bite of the stomach of the corpse of Vice President Fred March. His razor-sharp teeth ripping through the flesh with ease. It is a process he has repeated over and over to each of the corpses in the bio lab. He doesn't understand why he is doing it exactly just that it needs to be done. He rips out a chunk of flesh making sure to go deep enough to get some of the stomach lining as well. As he chews the flesh he sits on his haunches with his bloody hands across his knees. His golden eyes locked on the doors of the elevator. When he swallows this latest mouth full of flesh his body does something very strange. Archfiend doubles over and unleashes a very inhuman roar of pain as his body evolves on the spot.

There was one major upgrade that Doctor Tracey Todd and her team had added to the thing known as Archfiend that they told no one about. They injected him with a compound known as Z-99. The Z-99 compound was created for one purpose: To force evolution. The key to this change is varied biomass which is why Archfiend has had the urge to take chunks out of each corpse in the bio lab instead of only consuming one.

The change is over in mere minutes and when Archfiend stands, he has about fifty percent more muscle than he did before. He steps over the corpses of the Presidential staff and Secret Service agents as he makes his way to the elevator doors. Then he proceeds to rip the reinforced steel doors apart with terrifying ease. He could smell those waiting above and he was still starving.

Kevin stacked up on the wall watching as the Marines tried to get the heavy steel elevator doors open.

"Are you telling me that no one here has access to this fucking door?" asked Tom Jameson who is the acting Head of the Secret Service since Director Zachary Richards had went down with the President and wasn't answering his comms. "This is the most ignorant and unprofessional shit I have ever heard of."

Every available agent and Marine was down there now all chomping at the bit. The Marines were putting a laser cutter on the door since it had been no way to bypass it. Not even from the security and control room since it had been hacked by some group calling themselves Grayware. At first, Kevin had thought it was the Tide, but he had received warnings about an assault. The black phone in his pocket felt heavy and he wanted to do nothing more than put on his real uniform. But he was still undercover and needed to be now more than ever. Since the President and whatever was left of the government were most likely dead the Immortal would want to know what the hell had happened, and he wouldn't go back empty-handed.

"First we lose the country and now the President." Amy says from behind him. "All in two damn weeks. The Founding Fathers must be rolling over in their graves."

Kevin let out a snort and checks his watch. He feels Amy staring at the back of his head. He had been paired with her for a while now and he knew very well she is a hardcore patriot. She believed in America and most likely slept draped in the flag. What most impressed him is that she was not racist.

"Did I say something funny?" there is an edge in her voice.

Kevin just ignored her not caring to debate with her about the state of the country at this point. It was no need since the country was no longer what she idolized; it was what the Founding Fathers claimed to want America to be. A free nation where everyone was equal no matter their skin color, religion, or sexuality. He didn't need to defend that, and he never would it spoke for itself. Right now, all that he wanted to do was confirm what shit had hit the fan and try not to get sprayed. The Marines were about to activate the laser cutter when a horrible screeching sound began to echo through the corridor. Everyone had to cover their ears as the piercing sound ripped into their eardrums. Kevin knew it as the sound of tearing metal. He looks back down the hall at the elevator just in time to see doors being ripped apart like paper.

"Oh, fuck me." he pulls out his phone. "And fuck this shit."

He starts to put his finger on the scanner just as the doors explode out and something straight out of a nightmare comes exploding out of the elevator shaft and suddenly all Kevin sees is blood.

Archfiend explodes from the elevator shaft like a missile smashing the torn metal aside. He slams into a Marine driving her into the wall with so much force her body pops like a balloon spraying everyone nearby. Before anyone can react, he kills three more Marines with slashes of his blade-like claws. His movements are all perfectly calculated with no wasted motion. His claws open throats and spill guts. The first gunshots are not even aimed at him, they are caused by the spasming fingers of the dying Marines. The shots are wild and end up killing or injuring others nearby.

The massacre is surgical and terrifyingly fast as Archfiend was simply there one second and gone the next leaving bodies in his wake. There is nothing the Marine or Secret Service could do in the face of such inhuman violence, none of them stood a chance as he slaughtered them like armed cattle. He was about to rip the life from a tall white man in a suit when suddenly something hit him in the face with enough force to hurt.

Archfiend feels himself flying backward through the air. He regains his senses immediately and does a backflip midair. He lands on his feet and his claws dig deep gouges on the floor as he slides backward in the huge pool of blood. His golden eyes snap up and he sees a figure standing there. He is different from the others not wearing a suit or Marine battledress. He is in a black hoodie, camo pants, combat boots, and a red-eyed mask. Archfiend bares his teeth in a smile and spoke for the first time since waking up.

"Finally, a challenge." Archfiend says in a deep raspy voice so full of malice that death is a certainty for anyone who hears it. "I have not had a challenge in a very long time."
He begins to walk towards the figure. He wanted to savor this moment and he hoped that his hooded figure could survive long enough for him to get some satisfaction.

Kevin stands between the whatever the fuck this grey monster is and the surviving Marines and agents. As the thing starts to walk him down he feels his heart racing, but he doesn't take one step back. He is a Black Wolf, and his life is dedicated to protecting those who could not protect themselves. Right now, no one behind him could protect themselves from this thing. He looks back at the pale white face of Tom Jameson whom he had just saved from certain death.

"It's time for you to go Tom." Kevin says as he raises his mask to show his face.

Tom looks up at him in shock and Kevin smiles at him. He looks back at the rest of the agents as well making sure they can all see his face. None of them raise their weapons and neither do any of the Marines there. He nods to them all before looking at Tom again.

"I will hold it off as long as I can." he knows that his chances against this thing are not great. "You need to move fast and get as many out of here as you can. I am attempting to broadcast a distress signal, but it could be delayed because we are underground. You need to move now and keep moving."

He looks back at the approaching thing and sees that it is smiling at him like something out of a horror movie. He lowers his mask and activates his Last Stand Protocols. The Protocol deactivates the safety measures of his gear and strips his body of its natural limitations. He would need every ounce of speed, strength, and shield capacity he could get. He knows that even if this thing doesn't kill him, his body would not last long against the stress his gear would put on it. The built-in injectors flooded his body with both combat stims and nanites. The stims would allow him to push his body past it's limits and the nanites would work to keep him alive as long as possible. Kevin let out a grunt of pain as he feels the drugs and machines flood his bloodstream.

"Go now!" Kevin yells as he charges the grey monster.

The monster runs forward as well and even in his amped-up state, Kevin knows he is still outmatched here. The thing swings a black clawed hand at his head and Kevin ducks the blow. He had Force-Gloves at full power the first time he hit this thing and it had shaken it off like it was nothing. This time all of his gear and his entire body were at full power. So, when he drives an uppercut up into the thing's ribs the force of the blow slams it into the stone wall so hard the wall it cracks. Kevin cocks back his other fist and drives the second punch into the side of its face. The reinforced concrete gives way and the creature is driven through the wall and into an office. Kevin looks back at the stunned faces of the Secret Service and Marines who are still standing there like a bunch of idiots.

"I said go you dumb fucks!" he pointing in the opposite direction. "Run now, I can't-"

The grey monster shoots back out of the hole like a cannonball. It tackles Kevin with so much force he felt bone break and organs rupture even before they smashed through the opposite wall. His vision dimmed and when it came back, he found himself staring up at the cruel smile of the monster. Its golden eyes were glowing as it glared down at him. The pain ripping through his body was so intense it took every ounce of willpower just for him to stay conscious. His heads-up display is covered in warning telling him just how fucked up he is. One attack was all it had taken.

The thing reaches down and rips the mask off Kevin's faces. It examines it and then tosses it to the side like trash. Then it lowers bringng its face nose to nose with his.

"That was disappointing."

"Sorry about that but don't worry I called someone who will take you apart." Kevin says as he gives the creature a bloody grin.

The monster grins back at him and then raises a black clawed hand.

"I highly doubt that."
The claw comes down and Kevin McKenzie's face disappears.

Archfiend looks down at his latest kill. He was truly disappointed even though the man had managed to injure him superficially. He had cracked his ribs and dislocated his jaw. Both of the injuries had already healed which surprised him. He didn't know what all they had done to him, but it worked well. His hunger was still there but not as bad as it had been. His mind had cleared some allowing him to consider his situation. The taste of a challenge the Disappointment had given him sparked a new need that overpowered even the hunger, but the hunger was still there.

He reaches down and pulls what was left of the Disappointment's brain from his broken skull. He sits on his haunches and starts to eat as he listens to the sounds of the rest of the cattle attempt to escape him. He considers going after them but decides to consume biomass from the ones he had already killed first. This was by no means mercy, he just wanted to give them a chance to make this a challenge. He stands up and leaves the body of the Disappointment to continue his feast. He figured it would give his prey about a five-minute head start. It brought back memories of stalking through the sweltering, bug-infested jungles of Vietnam. He even started whistling a tone as he ate. It was the same tone he whistled back then right before he slowly pushed his blade into a gook.

Angela Deckland paced around the Presidential safe room. Her mood getting worse by the minute. She was the First Lady of the United States of America and yet she had been manhandled and then shoved into this room with no explanation. Ever since they arrived at Area 51 that had been the story of her life. No respect, not from her husband or the Secret Service that was sworn to protect her and her family. Gerald had been cheating on her for years with Lana, he didn't even bother to hide the affair from her anymore. He just spent the night in Lana's quarters instead of theirs. When she saw him the next morning and asked him where he had been, he would simply tell her with Lana. He did not even bother to make up a lie about being in a meeting anymore. With everything that was happening she might have believed him. What really pissed her off is the fact that she could not even pursue her own affair with Agent Tom Jameson. It had been hard enough in past but now with everyone living under each other it is impossible and if Gerald ever found out well it would not have ended well for her or her lover. Now, she did not even know if Gerald was alive or dead. When all of this was over, she would make sure that asshole Kevin McKenzie went to the shittest posting available.

Her seventeen-year-old daughter Whitney was curled up in the bed quietly sobbing and her fifteen-year-old son Maxwell's head was buried in his game as usual. She let out a sigh of frustration as she pulls a bottle of water from the fridge. Just as she is about to open it the steel door to the safe room opens and Tom runs in. At first, she is so glad to see him then she sees the look on his face and her heart skips a beat. The chaotic noises from outside suddenly flood the room and Tom grabs her arm hard and starts to drag her towards the back of the safe room.

"Ouch Tom let me go damn it and tell me what is going on!" Angela screams but he ignores her.

Behind her, two other agents grab both her kids and follows them. They reach a blank wall and Tom opens a hidden panel revealing a keypad. He punches in a code and a section of the wall opens revealing a tunnel. There is a pod that Angela recognized as a bullet pod sitting there. This was her second term as First Lady and she had been through all the security trainings dozens of times. This pod would get her and her children to a safe point that would be miles away from whatever danger they were in. That is when she realized things were far worse than she could have imagined. She remained silent as Tom and the other two agents pulled her family to the pod. Tom opened it revealing five seats inside. Angela, Whitney, and Maxwell were all secured first. Then Tom turned to the other two agents and give them orders.

"Get them out of here and keep them safe. If you can contact the Black Wolves and ask them for protection. Tell them what happened here and tell them the President is dead."

Angela felt a knife in her heart as she heard the words. Both of her children started to sob, and she did not know what she could say. The other two agents got into the pod and one of them got behind the controls. Angela just looked at Tom as he backed away from the pod. He raised a hand and gave her a small sad smile. Then without a word he turned and ran back through the doorway closing it behind him. The pod closed and five seconds later it took off down the tunnel like a bullet. Angela closed her eyes and the tears started as she finally accepted that her life as she knew it was over.

Tom Jameson is running for his life; the screaming and gunfire had started up again meaning that thing was on the hunt again. He had ordered his people to make a break for it and save whoever they could. Many of them had just gone for the elevator banks not caring to save anyone but themselves. He did not blame them for that at all after seeing that fucking monster he knew that the only chance they had of living was running. He had watched Kevin McKenzie throw himself at that monster just to give them a chance to getaway. It was the bravest thing he had ever seen, and he felt like a coward for running. For the first time, he understood what the Black Wolves stood for. He could not call any group terrorist when they had a man that brave amongst them. He made a promise to himself that if he survived this, he would find a way to join them and make sure that Kevin is remembered.

He turns a corner heading for the east elevators. He sees a group of civilians ahead of him being escorted by some Marines. They make a right turn at a T junction and then all he hears is screaming. He watches as the civilians come back around the corner with terror written all over their faces behind them the body of a Marine flies past disappearing down the hallway. Then a vision straight from Hell steps into view.

The thing had gotten even bigger now standing nearly seven feet tall. Its body was more muscular and on its head are two three-foot-long curved black horns. Tom watched in horror as the thing dropped to all fours before launching itself forward goring a fleeing man and woman through the back. Then it stood up straight letting them both scream in agony as they hung from its horns which were now driven into the stone ceiling. The thing laughs as it reaches up and tears them both off its horns, they are torn in half as it does this. It takes a bite out of each before throwing them to the side like trash. The thing is covered in blood now and has entrails hanging from it like decorations. It walks towards Tom it's horns carving trenches in the stone ceiling as it does. The hallway gets darker with every light it breaks.

Tom suddenly realizes that he is standing alone against the monster. The civilians had passed him up and now he stood alone in the hallway watching as the glowing golden eyes got closer and closer. He remembered how Kevin had charged the thing down and how brave he thought that was. Now, as the thing approached him, he realized how utterly insane it had been. Tom drops his gun and runs in the other direction realizing now that he wanted to live more than anything. He wasn't a hero, and he wasn't insane. Why hadn't he gotten into that bullet pod? He should've left that bitch and her brats in that room and taken the pod for himself or at least he should've been one of the agents with them. But no, he had stayed behind to try and be a hero. Tom was about to turn the corner when a horn slammed through his back and out of his chest. He was dead before his body was smashed through the wall by the charging monster.

Archfiend backs up pulling his horns from the wall and letting the coward's decimated body slide off. He stands up and let his horns pierce the ceiling once again as he glares down at the mutilated corpse. He gives it a contemptuous kick sending it flying down the corridor. The one thing he hated most in the world were cowards. He would not take a bite out of that body no matter how much the hunger nagged him. It was unforgivable for a warrior to drop their weapon in the face of an enemy. When he was known as Norman Pope, he would have taken pleasure in killing the coward slowly. Now, as Archfiend, he would settle for the most satisfyingly brutal.

He breathes in deep taking in the smells of prey all around him. He smiles and starts to move towards the closest group. He knew someone would escape to the surface and he was fine with that. When it was time he would do so as well. It was time for the world to experience the fear that everyone experienced when he hunted the jungles of Vietnam. With every transformation, he is stronger, faster and the hunger lessens. As the hunger lessens and his mind sharpens his taste, his old pleasures come back. He would make the deaths of those left here very slow and he would savor their agony before he savored their flesh.

The words of the Disappointment still echoed in his mind.

"Sorry about that but don't worry I called someone who will take you apart."

Archfiend lets out a chuckle and wonders what he would find waiting for him on the surface. They were considering waking him up for something. That was their mistake, and he would be the nightmare of whoever or whatever waited beyond this tomb. He starts to whistles as he continues his hunt.

CHAPTER 14

"So, let me get this straight you are going to Area 51 to fight what is obviously a fucking science experiment gone wrong at best and possibly a fucking demon at absolute worst?" Tyanna asked for the fourth time since I shared with her what was happening.

I am currently standing in the research and development lab located on the thirty-third floor of Tide Tower. All around me are some of the smartest minds in the world working on projects that will change it one day. I am standing in a chamber as robotic arms work to finish equipping me with my power armor. Tyanna, Zephrah, Craig, and my Head of Development Ahanti Parker all stand around the chamber watching. The two Elites are both in their full armor and merely stand in silence while I am prepared. Tyanna and Ahanti are taking turns telling me how stupid I am being.

"You are walking into a situation you have little to no real information on past one video." Ahanti says as she checks the status of my armor on her tablet. "I understand that you lost one of your Wolves and you are angry Bryson, but you are charging headfirst into a situation you don't understand. You don't know what that thing is or what it is capable of."

"You say you respect the opinions of black women." Tyanna says pointing at Ahanti. "She is one of the smartest women in the world period and she is black. She is telling you that you are being stupid, maybe you should listen to her."

The last piece of my armor is secured, and the chamber opens. I step out and the armor hisses as it calibrates itself. My armor is much more advanced than anything my Wolves wear. It is ten times more powerful as well and would kill most anyone else who tries to wear it. Unlike the enhanced uniforms worn by the soldiers of the Black Wolves or the armor worn by the Elites which are made for peacekeeping and lightning assaults, this armor is made specifically for war. I am already a large man at 6'4 and nearly three hundred pounds of muscle. With the armor my height is nearly seven feet and my weight is nearly a thousand pounds. My strength and speed which are already inhuman are enhanced even further.

"I understand you are both very much against this and I am sorry." I test the armor's mobility. "But this isn't something I can avoid. I have said and done a lot of things, now I have to back them up. Sitting by while a monster crawls out of a pit to massacre the state of Nevada and/or bring on the apocalypse isn't exactly good leadership."

"Neither is being eaten and/or dragged off to Hell." Tyanna says. "I am pretty damn sure being Immortal won't help you in either case. You own the American military, why can't you just hit it with a missile?"

"Because it's a bunker designed to withstand a nuclear blast first of all." Zephrah says speaking for the first time. "Second, it is Area 51, and we have no idea what they may have been working on in there. Now, we could drop a bunker buster or two or possibly release a plague that turns everyone on earth into vampire octopi or some other shit."

"While that makes perfect sense I still object." Tyanna says. "Oh, and it is octopuses, not octopi."

"I am aware, but I refuse to use a word that sounds that stupid." says Zephrah. "Now, can we go before someone decides to call whatever the fuck is living on Mars?"

I look at both her and Craig knowing that what I am about to say is going to piss them off as well.

"You won't be going with me." I say quickly as I move past them.

Not fast enough though because I have to stop short, so I don't trample Zephrah who is suddenly in front of me. She is glaring up at me with a sudden and intense rage in her eyes that leaves no question of what she would like to do to me.

"You want to run that by me again?" her voice as cold as ice. "Because I could have sworn, I just heard you say we aren't going. But I know I didn't just hear you say that because obviously, that would mean you have lost whatever the fuck is left of your mind. Also, I don't think you will enjoy me cutting off both your legs and beating you into a coma with them."

"Wait, what?"

"Hey Zephrah come on you have to-" Craig starts to move towards her but comes up short when she turns her glare on him. "Never mind, good luck boss."

"Yeah, thanks for nothing." I look down at my second in command. "Zeph, I can't bring you in this with me because the truth is, I don't know what this it. I haven't lost my mind, my child, I am always thinking of what is best for the family and the world we have started to rebuild. If anything happens to me, you will be the one who continues the dream. I have groomed you for this since you were thirteen years old and you are the only one, I trust to keep this going."

The heat in Zephrah's eyes cools some and she turns away. I hear an almost inaudible sniffle.

"Are you crying?"

"No, my allergies are acting up." she says as she wipes her eyes.

"But you don't have-"

"Shut up Craig."

Craig suddenly finds something on the floor very interesting. Tyanna steps up in front of me and I look to her expecting to see more anger but instead, I only see a need. I go down on one knee and gently put my armored hands around her waist. I lift her slowly until we are face to face. She puts hands on both sides of my face and pulls me in for a kiss. It seems to last forever and when it finally ends my heart is racing. She continues to hold my face and look into my eyes.

"I still don't want you to go but I understand why you feel you have too." she caresses my face. "But listen to me closely and hear me well. If you don't come back to me, I will come and find you. Believe me when I say you will regret it."

"I will be back, that is a promise." I put her down and stand up. "Now, for the part, you really aren't going to like. I will need to get there fast."

I turn around and look at Ahanti who takes off her glasses and rubs her eyes.

"Bryson, it still needs to go through more testing." Ahanti says her voice full of exasperation. "We have only had one human trial and that was only ten miles away."

"But it was successful, and you sent a monkey from here to the California lab."

"You are not a damn monkey Bryson; you are the leader of an eighty-million-man army that has conquered the most powerful nation the world has ever known." She fights to keep her voice calm. "You are asking me to put you in a machine that will tear you apart and send you seventeen hundred miles away."

"Excuse me what now?" Tyanna asked and from the tone of her voice, I can tell I am about to have yet another debate.

After another thirty minutes of pleading my case with these women and absolutely no help from Craig. When I say no help, I mean this asshole faked a comm call and left. I will be kicking his ass later. I finally made it to the teleportation platform.

"I just want to say for the record if you end up fused to a wall, I am in no way responsible." Ahanti says as she enters coordinates into the machine's computer. "I have it locked in. Are you sure you want to do this?"

"Yes, I am sure." I say trying to avoid the glares of Tyanna and Zephrah. "I am ready whenever you are."

"Hold it." Tyanna says as she walks over. "If you are doing this, you can at least show the world what you are willing to risk for them."

She holds out a case and he takes it. He knows it is full of mini drones that will transmit directly to U.N.N from there they would just have to start broadcasting.

"This could get pretty raw babe." I say.

"The last two weeks have been nothing but raw." she responds. "You say you want to build a world with truth, equity, and freedom as a backbone then you can't hide any of it."

She was right and I didn't argue as I took the case and stowed it. She puts her hand on mine and smiles up at me. We don't say anything further as she steps back from the pad. I look to Zephrah and she nods at me, but I can tell she is still not happy. I nod to Ahanti as I activate my suit's wolf's head helmet. The world goes black and then returns as my heads-up display comes online.

"Ready to go."

"Transporting in 3...2...1."

Ahanti hits the button and all I see is white light followed by a feeling of falling. This lasts for only a few seconds and then I feel solid earth under my feet. I let out a breath I didn't realize I was holding and look around. I am standing in the middle of the desert and in the distance sits Area 51.

"Good transport." I say into my comm. "About three miles away from the target location."

"We read you, Immortal." Zephrah replies over the comm . "Tyanna says the network is ready to receive your transmission. I have an Elite QRF on standby out of Vegas. They will be in the air ready to drop if needed."

"Understood, I'll deploy drones once on site."

I activate my suite grav-jet flight system and launch into the air. I straighten out and head towards the base. The sounds of gunshots and explosions reach me. I activate my vision enhancement and zoom in. The thing that comes into focus makes even my heart skip a beat. The monster has changed since I last saw it on video. It was huge easily seven feet tall with muscle that left no doubt of its power. It has two long curved black horns on its head, a pair of huge wings on its back, and a tail covered in black barbs. If it were not for the same flat face with the same shark-toothed grin and golden eyes I would have thought this was a totally different beast.

I watch as it tears through what remains of the military force on the base. Slaughter is the only way it can be described. The soldiers throw everything they have at the monster, but it is like kids throwing rocks at an attacking lion. Bullets, lasers, and explosions are all either dodged or completely shrugged off by the beast. I watch as it picks up a tank and throws it into an attack helicopter that was attempting to make a strafing run on it. The explosion threw troops below from their feet and the rain of flaming metal killed them. The beast leaned back and let out not a roar but a laugh taking joy from the death that it was causing. That pissed me off and I pushed my jets to the max turning myself into a missile and heading straight for the monster.

"Hey, you ugly son of a bitch how about you dance with me." my voice is amplified by my helmet.

The thing looks up at me seconds before I plow into its chest. We fly into the side of a building smashing through to the inside where we crash into vehicle after vehicle. One of them is a fuel truck and the resulting explosion throws us both through the air like rag dolls. I smash back through the wall and land hard outside carving a long grove into the stone. I let out a burst of my grab-jets and do a backward combat roll through the air landing on my feet. I look up just in time to see the thing flying up from the burning building covered in flames. It lets out a roar of anger not pain and its golden eyes lock on me. I reach back and pull out the case of mini drones. I put it on the ground and hit the activation button. The case opens and the drones fly out their systems linking up with the network's computers.

"I have contacted the target and I am officially ordering every Black Wolf to stay clear of this area." I say into the comm.

I don't have time to listen to the replies as the creature shoots at me like a missile. I break into a run and leap into the air firing my jets at full power. We crash into each other mid-air causing a massive shock way that throws us apart again. The force of it dims my vision a little and when it comes back to me, I see the creature coming at me again. I spin and hammer it in the face with a spinning back fist. As it is thrown to the side its tail slams into my chest with the force of a speeding eighteen-wheeler. We both slam into the ground with unbelievable force.

"Oh, fuck that one hurt."

My armor held and my body healed itself within seconds. I push myself to my feet and fly out of the crater landing hard on the stone. I find myself locking eyes with the monster watching as it's broken jaw pops itself back into place. One of its golden eyes had popped from the back fist. I watch as the eye heals perfectly and let out a low whistle.

"Well my friend I haven't seen anything like you since I looked in the mirror this morning." I say through my armor's speakers. "I wish we had met before maybe this could have been avoided."

I raise my right arm and a red energy blade comes out of my gauntlet. A red energy kite shield forms on my left as I put my armor into full combat mode.

"But you killed one of my sons and that I cannot forgive."

A smile forms across the things face and it points a black clawed finger at me.

"You are the one he called." the monster says in a voice dripping with malice. "The one who is supposed to take me apart. I am also betting that you are the one they woke me up to fight. What was your name? I listened to them talk about you, The Immortal, that was it! Such a stupid name almost as stupid as Archfiend."

"So, that is what you are called, Archfiend?" we began to circle each other. "They made you just to kill me?"

The thing laughs and it sounds like something from a nightmare. Who the fuck would wake up and decide they want to make something like this?

"Quite the ego you have Mr. Immortal." Archfiend says putting out his arms. "No, I was made to fight the enemies of America. In the sixties, it was the gooks and communists in Vietnam and today it's you. Don't get a big head friend you are just on a list. When I'm done with you, I'll move on to everyone else. No more leash, I make my list now. But I am going to enjoy you Mr. Immortal since I very much doubt, I will find anyone else who can challenge me."

Archfiend charges me and the thing is incredibly fast for something so big. I smile as I move just as fast. We meet in the middle and proceed to try and tear each other apart. I block a claw strike aimed at my head with my shield. I respond by stabbing at his chest with my energy blade. He dodges and spins away and his tail whips up into my shoulder sending me flying. I activate my jets and roll through the air landing on my feet. He is already on me when I look up a clawed hand is coming down at my head. I open my hand and send a gravity blast directly into his chest. He is sent flying back and lands hard on his back fifty feet away. I boost myself into the air and then boost directly down at him my sword aimed at his chest. He rolls away at the last second and my blade cuts into his back before being driven into the ground. He gets to his feet and leaps back. He lets out a pissed off hiss at me and I laugh in his face.

"What's the matter Archie, you seem mad." I pull my blade out of the ground and stand up. "I thought you wanted a challenge well here I am the biggest challenge you will ever face."

I check my armored diagnostic screen and see that it's repair systems are keeping up with the damage. My body is doing its repairs letting me keep up with the pace and brutality of this fight.

"You see if your goal is to eat the people of this world then you will have to go through my Wolves to accomplish that. For you to get to my Wolves, you will have to go through me. I can tell you now Hell will freeze over before you ever get through me. I am The Immortal, and this world is mine. You should've stayed in your hole."

"I'll rip you apart you arrogant piece of shit!" Archfiend bellows spreading his wings.

"Not before I take your soul bitch!" I prepare my grav-jets.

I realize us insulting each other like two teenage boys fighting on the playground may seem childish but men will be men. Seven years or seven thousand, we never really grow up. We both launch into the air taking our fight to the sky.

In the air, he is even faster, and he takes the advantage in combat. He comes at me straight on in the air, and I am forced to rely completely on my armor's flight system instead of a combination of both my natural abilities and my armor's capabilities. They are not enough to keep up with the bioengineered nightmare. He slams into me with a massive shoulder and follows it up with a right hook to my helmet that rattles my brains. The energy skin-shield that has kept my armor mostly intact throughout this fight is reaching its limit and I get a warning of imminent collapse. Archfiend continues his brutal assault with a spinning tail whip that I managed to block with my kite shield. The force of the impact still sends me flying and I feel something tear in my shoulder. I am still spinning when Archfiend slams into my back and starts to drive me towards the ground. His face is right beside my helmet when he speaks.

"What nothing else to say?" he asked as we started to accelerate towards the ground. "I am going to enjoy peeling what is left of you out of that armor and devouring you."

Warning signs on my heads-up display told me they were reaching terminal velocity and under ten thousand feet to do something about it, so I do something about it.

"Apex Mode." I yell and my heads up display suddenly blink out and my armor starts the process of transforming.

Most of the extra plating explode off of it knocking the Archfiend off of me and cutting my weight by sixty percent. A pair of red energy wings form on my back halting my descent almost immediately. The sudden stop would've killed anyone else but for me, it just hurts like hell.

My heads-up display comes back online and now displays "Alpha Mode" in the upper right-hand corner. In this mode, my armor looks a lot like the armor of my Elite with enhancements that only my body can handle. It sheds both power and protection for a massive increase in speed both in the air and on the ground. The weapons system also reflects this change of priority. Instead of a sword and shield, two sets of two-foot-long triple laser claws form over my hands and laser spikes on the soles of my feet. The grav-jet system in this armor is Gen Two. It has none of the safety functions of the Gen One system and allows for ninety percent more speed. The g-forces this produces would turn a normal person inside out. My healing ability will be hard-pressed to keep up with the damage I am about to inflict on myself. I look up and see Archfiend floating down towards me slowly.

"Sorry about that I wasn't dressed for the occasion." I say. "Shall we start this dance again? This time I'll lead if you don't mind."

"You get more arrogant by the second." Archfiend says as he stops about fifty feet above me. "I would have to guess I am dealing with a nigger. The only race of animal I ever met that was too uppity to understand their place no matter how much you beat the lesson into them. You know in Nam they were the only vermin I enjoyed killing more than gooks. The way they screamed when I cut into them was magnificent. You know I want to hear that again and scream for me nigger!"

He comes at me with that same terrifying speed. Then I am behind him, I watch as he cuts through the air where I was. He looks around in utter confusion.

"I was going to end this quickly." he spins around and looks up at me. "But you had to go and be a racist asshole."

I retract my faceplate to let him see my face. We lock eyes and study each out for a moment. My faceplate goes back on and I let out a sigh.

"You know what I still will." I force down my anger. "It is what I taught my children to do and it is what I will do. People like you don't deserve our anger. You just need to be erased from the world as quickly as possible. So, if you pray then I advise you to start. Within the next five minutes, you will be dead."

Archfiend starts to laugh but I cut it short as I shoot forward ramming both my hand claws through his chest. His eyes go wide as we plummet towards the ground. I spread my wings about twenty feet up pulling my claws out as I stall, letting him smash into the stone alone. I float down and land without a sound waiting. Three seconds later he explodes out of the smoke charging at me I sidestep him and kick him in the gut. He is sent flying away and he lands with a roll. He gets up holding his side which now has a crater in it where my kick smashed his ribs. I notice the cauterized wounds in his chest are closing. I wait and watch as the crater in its side pops back out with a sickening crack and take note of the seven-second delay.

"You should stop wasting your time, you are only making this worse on yourself." Archfiend says the malice in his voice increasing. "Those little claws of yours are only pissing me off. I am going to pull your limbs-"

I am on him again slashing as I dance around him. He tries to hit me but only cuts through the air as I cut into him over and over again. When I am done, I return to my starting point. I watch as he steps back with multiple cauterized wounds all over his arms, torso, and legs. I bite back my pain as my body repairs the multiple injuries, I just caused myself. Archfiend lets out an enraged roar and comes flying at me full speed, leap into the air at the last second and land on his back. I slashed down with both hands and sever his wings at the point where they meet his back. Both of them come off and he crashes to the ground. I leap from his back as he rolls across the stone and slams into the front of a building going through the stone wall like it was paper.

I land gracefully and watch the hole for a moment waiting for the thing to get back up. I look around and see the mini drones floating around catching the fight from every angle. I wonder how much of it they have been able to keep up with. I sidestep just in time to dodge a length of rebar that flies past at my head like a spear. I look back and see Archfiend standing in the hole with a second and third length of rebar in his hands. He looks horrible with half his face stripped away allowing teeth and bone to be seen from where his flesh use to be, both of his huge black horns are broken stubs, and more flesh has been stripped from different areas of his body. He launches the second length of rebar, but I am already on him and it flies through the air over my head. He looks down at me a second before I bury my claws in his guts and fly up cutting him open from his pelvis to collar bone. I flip in midair and come back down repeating the attack in the other direction. I land in front of him as he stumbles backward, his healing ability having difficulty keeping up with the damage. I don't plan on giving it a chance to even try as I raise my laser claws to full power. I shoot forward and drive both hand claws into his neck and both foot claws into his chest. The force of impact drives him to the ground. I retract my faceplate so I can look him in the eyes.

"Archfiend, you have been marked for execution by my order." I say with a tone of finality in my voice. "You know your crimes so I will not state them. May your soul travel quickly to its resting place."

He tries to let out a gargled roar, but I rip the blades through his thick neck decapitating him. His huge body bucks and spasms under me. I stay crouched on his chest until it stops. I watch waiting to see if it would attempt to regenerate but it lays still. Just for good measure I jump off the body, I retract my claw, grab a length of rebar and drive it into its severed head pinning it to the concrete.

"Holy fucking shit!"

I promptly fall on my ass and retract my entire helmet. The fresh air on my face feels better than sex. I fall back on my elbows and let out a breath of utter exhaustion. This was the first time in a very long time that I can honestly say I am tired. I close my eyes for a moment and when I open them, I see a drone hovering right in my face. I give it one of my trademark grins and then a thumbs up. Then, I promptly passed out.

Epilogue

I stand on the rooftop of the building that is now known as The Immortal Tower in the center of Atlanta. The city is alive again and it lights up the night.

Six months have passed and most of the world has surrendered to the Tide and the new order it has created. There are still hold outs and even pockets of resistance within those who have surrendered. What exactly they are resisting no one truly understands but they are allowed to speak their minds as long as they do it peacefully. Anyone who puts innocent lives in danger are put down hard.

My Wolves have taken over the governments and are working to link them all together. The process is going smoothly, and the worldwide network grows daily. The harder task will be rebuilding the broken parts of the world and those who live in them. Places like; Mexico and Columbia which has been run by the cartels for nearly a hundred years, Iraq and Saudi Arabia which have been labeled terrorist states since the turn of the century, Africa which has been considered the poorest continent on earth for generations, and the list goes on. Broken places and broken people all looking to us to deliver on the promises I made. Failure is not an option and my days are always busy now. I force myself to step away from it all and let my mind rest. A tired mind makes bad decisions, and all of my decisions affect the lives of billions of people now.

I am starting to consider one of the more recent issues to come across my desk when I feel arms wrap around my waist. I smile when Tyanna lays her head on my back.

"Hello, my love how are you feeling?" I ask as I slowly turn to face her.

I look down at her and see that she is wearing a long white dress that goes down to her knees and a pair of sandals. She steps back and smiles up at me as she takes my hand and guides it to her round belly which holds our unborn child. The fight with Archfiend was the toughest of my life and it forced some sort of evolution. Side note: the fight is the most watched television broadcast in history. Long story short I can have kids now. Believe me, it shocked the hell out of me too when Tyanna told me she missed her cycle. I won't lie I almost asked who the father was? Since I still have my head, I obviously didn't.

"Better now." she raises my hand to her lips and kisses it. "I woke up and you weren't in bed."

I look down at the diamond engagement ring on her finger. I had asked her to marry me a week prior and she has not stopped smiling since. She is a part of the new government as well having taken the position of Head of Media Relations, meaning she decides how much of my life is for public consumption.

"Looking out over your empire?" she asked me teasingly.

Over the last month many people have started calling me The Immortal Emperor and the name has caught on. Tyanna and Zephrah never miss an opportunity to remind me of it and I have even started to receive messages addressing me by the title.

"Yes, you know I can't help myself." I say with a grin. "I have to survey all that is mine and bask in the glory that is me."
She laughs and slaps my chest.

"Whatever dummy, the only thing I will be basking in is the back of my eyelids." she leads me back into the penthouse. "You can be Emperor later; I need my cuddles now."

I don't struggle as she leads me back to our bedroom. The world could survive without me for a while.

Made in the USA
Columbia, SC
21 November 2020